QUEENS OF CYBERSPACE

THE FLOATING EYE

Clancy Teitelbaum

EPIC
Press

The Floating Eye
Queens of Cyberspace: Book #3

Written by Clancy Teitelbaum

Copyright © 2016 by Abdo Consulting Group, Inc.

Published by EPIC Press™
PO Box 398166
Minneapolis, MN 55439

Printed in the United States of America.

Cover design by Laura Mitchell
Images for cover art obtained from iStockPhoto.com
Edited by Jennifer Skogen

LIBRARY OF CONGRESS CATALOGING-IN-PUBLICATION DATA

Teitelbaum, Clancy.
The floating eye / Clancy Teitelbaum.
p. cm. — (Queens of cyberspace; #3)
Summary: It's been a month of in-game time since the girls were trapped in Io, and
while Mikayla, Suzanne, and Brit have grown more powerful, their enemies grow
more dangerous instigating war. When the conflict comes to a head, the girls will
have to take responsibility not just for themselves, but for an entire kingdom.
ISBN 978-1-68076-199-3 (hardcover)
1. Friendship—Fiction. 2. Computer games—Fiction. 3. Internet—Fiction. 4.
Virtual reality—Fiction. 5. Cyberspace—Fiction. 6. Video games—Fiction. 7.
Young adult fiction. I. Title.
[Fic]—dc23

2015949425

EPIC
Press

EPICPRESS.COM

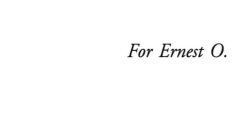

For Ernest O.

Chapter 1

"Where are they?" Suzanne whispered. She lay on her stomach, flat against the earth. She'd been lying there since the sun was up, waiting for the convoy. Now the sun was down and it was beginning to look like they wouldn't show.

Peering through a bush, she scanned the shadows on the road again. The only movement she saw came from Brit and Mikayla's player icons, lazily twirling over their hiding spots.

Mikayla perched in a tree branch, completely still, staring off into the distance for any sign of the convoy. Suzanne could barely find the silhouette of her friend. Mikayla could see farther than the other girls; she was a Ranger. They were hiding in case any Rangers were accompanying the convoy.

A nearby shrub rustled impatiently. That was Brit. She was a Fighter, a class that emphasized strength over stealth. That meant it was easier for Suzanne and Mikayla to hide Brit than it was for Brit to hide herself. Hours earlier, Suzanne and Mikayla had draped foliage over her, hoping the darkness would make Brit's camouflage convincing.

Suzanne stifled a yawn. The Altairi convoy should have shown up by now, according to the intel they'd got from Libra. They were bringing weapons and armor from Altair to the Altairi troops stationed in Pyxis. Maybe the convoy ran into some monsters and the monsters handled the girls' job for them. *That would be nice*, Suzanne thought, *we could go back to camp and sleep.*

"Here they come!" Mikayla hissed, the word cutting through the night like a knife. The shrub rustled again, Brit readying herself for combat. Suzanne drew a dagger from her inventory and waited for the NPCs to come into view.

It wasn't long before Suzanne could hear the sounds of a pushcart and footsteps approaching. Like Mikayla, Suzanne saw the icons first, gray diamonds twirling over the heads of the shadowy figures, signifying they were NPCs, not monsters or other players. She counted six of them in total. Easy enough.

A dozen meters away from Brit's shrub the convoy halted. The NPC at the front took a few cautious steps forward, staring at where Brit was hiding. *Oh great*, Suzanne thought, *they brought a Ranger.*

High up in her tree Mikayla knocked on the trunk three times—the signal. Brit burst out of the shrub with her halberd raised, charging down the convoy. The NPCs fell into a defensive formation immediately. There were two enemy

Fighters—every bit as big as Brit—the Ranger, and a trio of Sellswords.

All initial classes. And Suzanne had been worried this was going to be a hard fight.

Even if the Altairi Fighters were as big as Brit, they clearly weren't on her level. Her mailed fist punched in the face of the first one, slamming him backwards into the tree Mikayla was perched on. Mikayla dropped down from her branch and administered a quick finishing blow with her estoc.

The second Fighter swung her war hammer at Brit, but Brit grabbed the shaft of the weapon, diverting the blow into the dirt. With a wrench of her wrist she ripped the hammer out of the Altairi's hands, tossing it off into the foliage.

Meanwhile Mikayla had thrown herself at the nearest Sellsword. She slashed at the Sellsword's sword arm, disabling her enemy before a quick slash to the throat finished the NPC off. Disarm then kill, disarm then kill. The girls had logged enough hours of combat that it had been reduced to those two easy steps.

The disarmed Fighter backed away from Brit and into range for Suzanne. She jumped out of hiding and planted her dagger into a weak spot in the Fighter's armor. Disarm then kill. Suzanne remembered her first fights in Io, when the girls struggled to defeat low-level enemies and monsters. True, they were at lower levels themselves, but they were also going about the fights all wrong. Combat in Io wasn't about pulling off the flashiest combos or using the sweetest finishing moves. It was, Suzanne concluded as she twisted her dagger, about outthinking NPCs, understanding the patterns in their attacks and taking advantage of their predictability. Especially against these weaker opponents.

Suzanne let the Fighter's lifeless body fall from her grasp. It hit the earth and exploded into pixels, like all game objects did when they ran out of health.

The remaining two Sellswords and the Ranger ran off the road into the woods, hoping the darkness would hide them from the girls. Suzanne fought the urge to roll her eyes. It was a bit silly for the Altairi to try hiding when she could clearly see the gray icons floating over their heads.

"I want the Ranger," Mikayla said. "I'm like a hundred XP behind the two of you and we always get more for Rangers. A Sellsword's what, fifty XP?"

"Whatever," Suzanne replied, "let's just finish them and get back to the camp."

The Sellsword Suzanne went after stayed hidden as she approached. No matter. Suzanne walked past the bush as if she didn't know he was there. But as soon as he was behind her she whirled around and threw a dagger into the foliage. The Sellsword tumbled out of the bush, clutching his side where the hilt of Suzanne's dagger protruded. Suzanne was on him in a flash, finishing him off with a few quick stabs. He had a beard, she noticed, as his body reduced to pixels and the pixels scattered away into nothingness. NPCs didn't often have beards.

Brit emerged from the trees nearby; her Sellsword hadn't been a challenge either. They followed the sound of clashing swords and came upon Mikayla dueling the Altairi Ranger. To Suzanne, Mikayla always looked like she was dancing when she fought. She held her estoc close to her body to block any strikes. Then she'd lunge out quickly to strike and nimbly sidestep any return swings.

The Altairi Ranger fought like he knew he was outmatched. Afraid, he swung wildly while Mikayla picked him apart. As her friend dodged a desperate thrust, Suzanne wondered how long Mikayla would take to finish him off. No matter who or what she was fighting, Mikayla always prioritized defense. Suzanne and Brit always had to heal after battles, but Mikayla usually escaped fights unscathed.

Which only added to the shock when Suzanne

saw the Altairi Ranger's blade stab into Mikayla's midriff and emerge on the other side.

Mikayla stumbled backwards in shock, dropping her estoc and clutching her stomach. The Altairi looked just as surprised as she did.

"No!" Brit shouted. She crossed the clearing in large steps and swung her halberd two-handed, lopping the Ranger's head off of his shoulders. Brit ignored the Ranger's loot drop, fretting over Mikayla.

Suzanne tore through her inventory, looking for a healing item. She found a potion Libra had given her and withdrew it. The bottle appeared in her hand and she ripped the cork out.

"I still have half my health bar left," Mikayla said, her voice a little weak. "I'm fine."

And Suzanne realized she was. No matter how visceral the animation, she had to remind herself that she was, after all, in a game. As long as the girls had even a shred of their health bars left, they could recover from basically any injury. All it took was healing items and time.

Still, no number of hours logged in-game would ever get Suzanne used to seeing her friend stabbed through the gut. Brit stooped and picked Mikayla up, carrying her over to one of the convoy's push-carts. The Altairis wouldn't need them anymore.

"I just zoned out," Mikayla explained once they were on their way back to camp, her health restored and the convoy looted. "He was basically finished but I got careless and I guess he saw his chance."

"What'd we get?" she asked, eager to change the subject.

Suzanne gestured back to the cart Brit was pulling. "Some medium-grade weapons, a couple of nicer axes, and spears. Some decent armor. It should help arm more units, but it's not really grade-A stuff."

"Since when is Altairi stuff grade-A?" Brit asked. Suzanne listened to her friends joke with each other, but in her mind she was still in the moment when the blade appeared on the other side of Mikayla's stomach. This was their life while they were trapped in Io. If they won, they kept on fighting and killing.

And if they lost? Suzanne still didn't know what would happen if one of them died. Best case scenario they'd log out and get to return to reality. But if they died they might also be sent into limbo, trapped between the game and reality. And there was always the chance that dying in-game meant something worse. What if dying in Io meant dying in the real world?

Suzanne pushed those thoughts away, back behind the locked door where she usually kept them. Tonight they had successfully raided an Altairi convoy and helped the Pyxians in their war. They were only a few levels away from reaching advanced classes, and then they'd be so tough no one could mess with them.

Chapter 2

As soon as the girls got back to camp, Mikayla split off to make the report to Libra and Brit went to drop off the loot at the Pyxians' armory. Suzanne said goodbye to her friends and stopped to stretch out a yawn. Barring any surprise attacks, she was free until the war meeting that afternoon. That left her the rest of the morning to do whatever she wanted.

She thought about sleeping—she had been up all night after all, stalking the Altairi convoy. But she wasn't tired and her health was fine so she kept walking past the tent she shared with Brit and Mikayla on the edges of the camp and headed into the center.

They'd been at this camp a week. The camp was situated a few hours' walk from the edge of Ion River, but not so far west as to get lost in the foothills of Pyxis. The forest where the girls ambushed the convoy provided a southern border. The trees grew thick enough that the Altairi couldn't surprise them with an attack from the south.

Sentries were posted to the north, east, and west—Rangers, like Mikayla, their high perception trained on the horizon, waiting for the army of Ramses to make its move. But the Altairi had become uncharacteristically defensive since Libra led her army down from the mountains to liberate Pyxis.

In fact, Suzanne realized, apart from grinding XP and intercepting the occasional convoy, the week they'd been camped here had been her most peaceful week since she'd been trapped in Io. The girls weren't prisoners or under attack. And while they were still on the same quest to escape the game, they were now pursuing that goal indirectly.

To log out, Suzanne needed to get to the Oracle Chamber in Altair's capital, Zenith City. But the girls were wanted for murder in Altair and were former prisoners of Altair's duplicitous king, Ramses. So to get back to Zenith City they were fighting alongside Libra, the queen of Pyxis, as she tried to free her land from Altair. And fighting alongside Libra meant fighting in the Pyxian Army, which meant doing what you were told, which meant that since no one had told Suzanne what to do this morning she was free to do whatever she wanted.

Which left the question of what she wanted to do.

She could pursue a skill. Back when she was testing the world of Io with a mouse and keyboard, before she used the TII to enter the game, she designed skills as a compliment to combat. Weaving and woodworking were skills your character could learn, but it took time. And the idea of spending all morning crouched over a pile of wood, slowly whittling away, was as repulsive to Suzanne as the thought of taking on the Altairi Army by herself.

Some skills were inborn. Troubadours started out the game masterful at whatever instrument they picked up. Rogues, the class that Suzanne belonged to, could pick locks starting at level one.

She'd envisioned skills as a way to flesh out a player's character. Sure, you might be playing the game as a Barbarian, but maybe between battles you sat down at a potter's wheel and went to work. But so many of those skills seemed useless now that she was in Io all the time. So what if you made the nicest pots? All you could do with a pot was break or sell it. The same went for most of the items that skills yielded. In a world where you got gold for killing monsters, making money by selling pots wasn't worth the time.

But not every skill crafted a useless item. Suzanne followed the sounds of clanging metal, as she often did when she had downtime at camp, to the tents where the smiths worked.

This was a skill she could invest in. The smiths were a motley assortment of melee characters. A Fighter and a Defender stood shoulder to shoulder with a Vanguard and a Paladin, hammering and tempering out the weaknesses in greaves, swords, and mail. They were as much a unit as any other in the army. The half-dozen NPCs assembled worked in harmony, executing the orders of their commander, the master smith Rigel.

By class Rigel was a Monk, but Suzanne never saw him fight. Still, he showed off his dexterity each time he picked up the hammer and tongs. Suzanne met the NPC after returning from her first convoy raid. She had tried to parry a Barbarian's two-handed swing with one of her daggers, more out of boredom than anything else. The impact of the blow was too great and the blade of her dagger snapped right off its hilt. After the battle, Suzanne found two new items—one for the blade and one for the hilt—and took them to the Pyxian smiths to see what could be done.

By the time she made it back to the forges, all the other smiths besides Rigel were off duty. The master smith immediately set to work reattaching the blade, talking to Suzanne as he did.

"It's good you saved both pieces. It'll be better that way."

"How so?" she asked.

"You've had this weapon a while, right? My guess is you probably maxed out on proficiency with it."

"Yeah," she said. "But doesn't that carry over to other daggers?" Having designed the weapon system herself, Suzanne was sure that it did. But she always liked to play a little dumb with the NPCs so she wouldn't seem impossibly knowledgeable to them.

But Rigel's answer surprised her. "No, they don't work like that. Once you max out proficiency on a weapon you're the master of that blade only."

He kept working as he explained, and by the time he was finished mending the dagger, Suzanne realized she had made a mistake while coding proficiency. From then on she had been sure to stick to one dagger for melee fighting and tried to find all her throwing daggers after each battle. And she made a point of visiting with Rigel as much as possible, so she could pick up more tidbits from the Monk. Over the past week, Suzanne had become a regular sight at the forges.

She greeted the now-familiar faces of the smiths. Rigel looked up from the plate mail he was working and smiled as Suzanne approached.

"Break another dagger?" he asked.

She shook her head.

"Well then, you can lend a hand."

Suzanne took the hammer Rigel offered her and squeezed between him and a burly Defender working on a helmet. To smith successfully, she had to strike the armor in the right place with the right amount of force at the right time. The armor glowed wherever she was supposed to hit it. Tempering weapons in Io was kind of like whack-a-mole, Suzanne thought, but she knew that was a reference none of the NPCs would get.

Aside from Rigel, most of the NPCs worked in silence. The Monk didn't have that luxury: he kept an eye on all the items being forged and was ready to offer advice or step in himself if he thought another character was botching the job.

"You're all wrong," he growled, grabbing the hammer out of Suzanne's hand. She continued to hold the tongs as he stared at the armor, waiting for a new forge spot to appear. Suddenly, the armor started glowing right below the neck. Rigel dealt a savage blow with the hammer, which Suzanne felt travel through the armor and up the tongs to her arm. The armor stopped glowing and a new forge spot appeared on the back. Satisfied, Rigel handed her the hammer back and watched as she tried.

Suzanne took her best shot, picturing Brit smashing down with her halberd. The hammer clunked off the armor, but the forge spot didn't disappear. Rigel hastily grabbed the hammer back and hammered out the forge spot.

Then he lifted the armor from the forge, examining the item. "When you fight," he said, "do you use your right hand or your left?"

"Both," she replied.

"Well, I suppose you're a Rogue." He squinted at the armor, examining it with his highly refined appraising abilities. "Rogues aren't known for their strength, after all."

Suzanne felt herself becoming frustrated. This was why she had gravitated toward computers and gaming as a kid, moving away from rec league soccer and other sports. She was a textbook indoor kid. It was frustrating to think that even in Io, she wasn't cut out for physical activity.

But there was no reason that should stop her. It didn't matter how strong she was if she was fast enough. She explained her idea to Rigel whose face lit up in a grin as soon as he heard it.

He held the iron to the forge like a vise while Suzanne grabbed two smaller hammers, usually used for more delicate work like circlets and visors. Once more, a forge spot started glowing on the plate mail, only this time Suzanne smacked it first with her right hammer and then with her left, just like she was attacking an enemy in battle. The forge spot disappeared upon the second hammer strike.

Rigel examined the armor again.

"Perfect," he said. "Couldn't have done it better myself. You're an odd one, Suzanne, no doubts about it. Never seen someone forge two-handed before."

She worked on armor the rest of the morning. Rigel set up an actual vise so he didn't have to hold what she was forging for her. With each item, Suzanne felt herself becoming more adept at smithing. The forge spots glowed brighter and longer and she struck with more precision. This wasn't like leveling up, where you reached a threshold and suddenly became stronger. She was cultivating a skill. To her, it felt like a more organic process.

She became immersed in the process. Soon she had repaired not only the plate mail but also a set of greaves, two sets of gauntlets, and a helmet. She looked up from the forge to see Leo loitering nearby, doing his best to not appear to be watching her.

Which of course was what he was doing. He was leaning against a tent post, the sleeves of his Pyxian robe rolled up on his arms. Leo was terrible at looking casual. Even in the Pyxian camp, surrounded by friends, his gray eyes were always alert, always looking for any sign of danger.

She hung up her hammers and slipped away from the forge. In the real world, she mused, she'd be sweatier and dirtier than gym clothes after spending all morning hammering away over a forge. But here in Io, she didn't even have a hair out of place.

He spotted her walking toward him and she

watched him go through a miniature panic attack. It was refreshing not to be the awkward one, for once.

"Hello, I, uh, wanted a chance to see you before the war meeting."

"Here I am," she said, weaving her fingers in with his. The gesture was undoubtedly alien to him—Suzanne had never seen NPCs holding hands—but its meaning was clear enough.

They walked into the rows of sleeping tents, away from the clamor of the smithing tent to where they could hear each other. She didn't know exactly what this thing was that she had going with Leo, but whatever it was, she was enjoying it.

"I heard you ran into some trouble with that last convoy," Leo said.

The memory of the blade stabbing through Mikayla flashed before Suzanne's eyes. She shrugged it off. "Nothing we haven't seen before," she said, trying to keep her voice casual.

Leo didn't seem to buy it. "I just . . . I just

want you to be careful. If anything happened to you . . . "

"What?" Suzanne wanted to ask. "What would you do?" But she swallowed those words. "We're big girls," she said instead. "We can take care of ourselves."

"I know that," he said. "But sometimes, the way you fight, it's like you don't even care about getting hurt. Like the enemy's attacks don't matter to you."

Suzanne stopped walking. Her fingers fell out of Leo's grasp. What he said, technically, was true. Suzanne kept her eyes on her health bar as she fought, but she was cavalier with her life until she was in the red. The pain she felt in this world was mental. Her real body was never hurt, but when she saw she was taking damage her brain reflexively told her to feel pain. Once she understood that, there was no reason for her to shy away from damage. She didn't realize any of the NPCs would notice.

"I know you want to get home," Leo continued, "but you shouldn't be so desperate. After all, once you make it home . . . "

This time Suzanne knew what he was going to say. But before they could continue their conversation further, bells rang out throughout the Pyxian camp. It was time to plan a war.

Chapter 3

Leo and Suzanne walked over to Libra's tent, where they met up with Brit and Mikayla. Suzanne's eyes flitted down to where Mikayla had been stabbed, but of course there was no sign of her injury. Suzanne told herself she was being silly: they were in a game where getting gutted was no big deal.

Together, the four of them ducked inside the tent. Six chairs flanked the long sides of a table and a thirteenth for Libra sat at the head. Mallon, Rigel, and Leo's twin sister, Lynx, were already seated along with the other high-ranking NPCs in the Pyxian Army.

Mallon winked at Suzanne and Suzanne waved back. She was an old NPC with silver hair and a silver whip coiled around her arm. Mallon was in charge of scouting for their campaign, and after Lynx, Leo, and Libra, she was the Pyxian Suzanne trusted the most. But she was engaged in a conversation with Rigel and turned back to continue it.

All the Pyxians wore robes, regardless of rank or class. Comparatively, Suzanne and her friends looked like they were expecting an attack at any second. Suzanne and Mikayla had leather armor equipped, and Brit always wore her plate mail.

"What were you up to?" Brit asked with a nod toward Leo as they slid into their seats.

"I was working with the smiths," Suzanne said.

"You're really grinding out a skill?"

Suzanne had to laugh; Brit sounded so incredulous. "It's fun. And Rigel knows tons about how the equip system works. I'm learning more and more about how the world functions."

"Whatever," Brit said. "Like you don't already know all that crap."

"Well, I think it's a good idea to work on skills," Mikayla said. "I'm sure you're becoming a great smith."

"Of course you think it's a good idea," Brit said, rolling her eyes.

The two of them broke into playful squabbling that lasted until Libra entered. As often happened when the Pyxian queen entered a room, the room fell silent. The NPCs and the girls stood as the queen crossed to her chair and sat down.

Libra wore none of the medieval foppery that Suzanne pictured a queen wearing. Like the other Pyxians, she wore a simple robe. The only mark of her station was the plain circlet crowning her head. But the way Libra spoke, the way she listened with a look of intense engagement—these were the undeniable markers that she was a ruler among NPCs.

"Friends," she began, "thanks to the efforts of

Brit, Mikayla, and Suzanne, the Altairi supply lines are devastated. Soon the Altairi will be fighting with broken spears and ragged armor and they will be no match for our forces."

"Not that they ever were," Mallon added.

Her words were met with mutterings of approval from around the table.

"Be that as it may," Libra continued with a smile, "now is not the time to get overconfident. We fight against a larger foe, one without mercy, and the instant we underestimate our enemy is the instant we lose this war."

Following that, each division head gave their report. According to Rigel, they had a good surplus of weapons and armor, especially considering what the girls had managed to loot from the Altairi convoys. Mallon reported that the main body of the Altairi force was camped to the northeast, their backs to the river. Mikayla spoke for the girls, giving a brief account of their most recent ambush, glossing over the part where she got stabbed.

"And now," Libra said, "Leo has asked for a chance to speak." Suzanne turned with the rest of those assembled to look at Leo, who was seated nearest the foot.

"I think," he said, rising to his feet, "that we're going to lose this war." Instantly the other NPCs began to speak up in protest but one look from Libra quelled their words.

"As long as Ramses has a kingdom," Leo continued, louder than before, "he has an endless number of Citizens to conscript into service. No matter how hard we fight, eventually we will be overwhelmed."

"What would you have us do?" Mallon asked. "Start conscripting our own Citizens?"

Leo shook his head. "We need to turn Ramses's people against him. For them, this war is a distant thing. We need to make it part of their reality. I suggest we launch a counteroffensive into Altair. It will split the focus of the Altairi Army and turn the Altairi citizenry against their king."

"Will it?" Lynx asked, her tone skeptical. "Won't that just legitimize all of Ramses's propaganda about us?"

"Who cares if we legitimize propaganda? We aren't the Altairi—we aren't going to murder Citizens," Leo spat back.

Lynx laughed. "Just rough them up then? Or were you planning on taking entire villages prisoner and holding them for ransom against their mad king?"

"We would take out the villages that produce the items for the Altairi forces. Without their smiths and apothecaries they won't be able to continue this war. They'll have to withdraw forces to defend their supply centers and then we'll be able to easily crush the Altairi that remain."

"But what are you going to do with those smiths and apothecaries?" Mikayla demanded, glaring at Leo. "What do you mean when you say you're going to take them out?"

"I will do what is necessary to protect Pyxis," he replied.

"This is not the first time I have heard these plans," Libra said before Mikayla could continue the argument. "And I am as disinclined to pursue them now as I was previously. But I know that my perspective is limited and so I agreed Leo could submit them to the War Council."

No one at the table seemed to be in favor of Leo's plan.

"It won't do," Mallon said. "We've got no eyes on Altair. Aside from a few sketchy maps, you'd be going in blind."

"Even so," Leo replied, "any damage we do over there will bring us closer to peace here. We must try, right, Rigel? Don't you think we should stop being so passive about winning this war?"

The old Monk scratched his chin thoughtfully. "Can't say myself. I like the idea of finishing this fight as fast as we can, but it won't do us any favors if we make ourselves more enemies for the future. Right now we're warring with Ramses and his army. I'd rather not add the Altairi people to that list."

"Very well," Libra said. "Then the matter is decided. We will not launch a counteroffensive into Altair and we will continue to fight for the liberation of our homeland."

"We haven't heard from everyone yet!" Desperation was creeping into Leo's voice. "Suzanne hasn't spoken on the manner and—"

"The last I checked," Libra said, cutting him off, "Libra, and not Suzanne, is queen of Pyxis. Her authority does not supersede mine. The matter is decided."

Chapter 4

"Wasn't I just doing this?" Suzanne muttered to herself. She crawled through the Altairi forest on her stomach, pulling herself forward with her arms. The scrub brush provided all the cover she needed. Tall trees blocked the moon and cast plenty of shadows to hide in.

She heard a sound off to her left. No doubt it was Carsten or Naveen, one of Leo's men. She knew none of them were Rogues, but she had hoped that they all weren't blunderers. If the constant sounds of broken twigs and rustling were anything to go by, she was the only one on this "stealth" mission capable of stealth.

And yet, she realized, part of her hoped they were discovered. Part of her hoped the Altairi posted guards and those guards possessed unusually high perception skills. Part of her hoped the mission failed.

Libra had forbidden it, this saboteur's errand. Was that what gave Suzanne pause? She shook the thought from her head and kept crawling forward, toward the distant torchlight of the village. *Before anything else*, she told herself, *we have to get to the village. Then we can figure out how to shut their forges down.*

But that thought did little to calm the uncertainty she felt. Leo's plan wasn't much of a plan. The council meeting ended shortly after Libra shut Leo down. He'd grabbed Suzanne's hand as she exited the tent, pulling her aside to somewhere they could talk without others listening.

"We're going ahead anyway," he said, breathless with his secret. "If my sister can't see reason then we'll prove it to her."

She should have argued with him, she knew. But she trusted Leo, more than any other NPC, so instead she merely asked, "Who's 'we'?"

He showed her. Besides himself there were Naveen and Carsten, both Pikers by class. Naveen wore a constant smile and laughed boisterously, perhaps too much so for a stealth mission. Carsten's long brown curls made him look more like a dog than an NPC, but Leo assured her they were two of his oldest friends. They were joined by Hollis, a small Fighter Suzanne recognized from working at the forge, and Shasta, a Monk who wore her hair in a long braid and carried no weapons. And, of course, Leo counted on Suzanne making the party six.

Six against how many? Leo had no idea. They were going in nearly blind, just as Mallon had warned them. What if there were twenty guards at the village? Fifty? Suzanne cursed herself for not thinking of these questions before she got into the boat and crossed over the Ion River to Altair. The boat was the same one Suzanne had used to first cross the Ion River, ferried by Leo and Lynx.

Lynx did not join them for this journey back. She had made her views on the matter clear enough in the council meeting. Suzanne realized that none of the Pyxians, besides Leo, had been at the council meeting. She wondered if they knew their mission had been forbidden, whether they openly defied their queen, or if Leo withheld that information from them.

Leo had urged Suzanne not to tell Brit and Mikayla. Suzanne knew Mikayla would say no, but Brit could have been convinced. The other four Pyxians were clearly old friends. No doubt they had fought together before and were comfortable in a party. Besides Leo, though, Suzanne had never even seen any of them fight. She would have felt way better fighting alongside one of her friends. But as soon as she agreed to join Leo and the others, they set off, leaving her no time to look for

Brit or to get to know her new party, aside from their names.

So now she was crawling through the Altairi forest on her hands and knees, freezing at the slightest sound, her hand twitching toward her dagger. After what felt like an hour in the undergrowth she reached the edge of the woods. Across a short meadow she saw the wall surrounding the town.

It was small, hardly larger than a village. Black smoke, blacker than the night, billowed out of the chimneys of the town, trailing upward into the sky. Even at night the forges burned. Halfway across the meadow was a sign. Illuminated by the moon, Suzanne read the name: RIVERFORGE.

She made out the shapes of the NPCs in the darkness and crawled toward them. The six of them gathered in the shadow of the trees.

In a whisper she asked Leo, "What now?"

The Pyxian prince looked from her to the others and back again. There was no uncertainty in his voice. "We'll circle around and jump the eastern wall. If they have any eyes, they'll be west, toward the river. They won't see us coming."

"And then what?" she asked.

"And then we stop the forge," he replied. "By any means necessary." He stared into her eyes. "Unless you have another suggestion?"

She didn't want to know what he meant by that. Suzanne felt like it was too late to back out, and she fell in behind Leo as they scurried through the darkness. Leo led the way, sticking close to the edge of the forest. Once they were well east of the town, he broke into a low run toward the wall.

As he had said, no eyes were on the eastern wall. The six of them crossed the meadow without any incident, stopping only to pull Carsten back to his feet after he stumbled in the dark and fell.

Suzanne felt along the wall for hand holds and began to climb up. Shasta, nimble as any Monk, climbed alongside her. But the rest of the NPCs couldn't scale the wall alone. Hollis and Naveen set their weapons down and boosted Leo up to the top. By the time he was atop the wall, Suzanne and Shasta had landed quietly on the other side. They crouched behind a house, waiting in the shadows for the others.

Leo pulled up Hollis after himself, and together the two of them lifted Carsten and Naveen. One by one they dropped down into Riverforge. Leo and Naveen landed well enough, but Carsten fell on his ankle and yelped in pain. His cry rang loud through the quiet night, but if any townsperson heard, they ignored it. Hollis landed like a sack of rocks.

The fact that no one had come worried Suzanne all the more. While Leo shimmied down, she crept out from behind the house to scout. Even if it was night, it made no sense for the streets to be this deserted. Yet everywhere she looked the blinds were drawn, shutters down and doors closed. It was as if the town was completely abandoned, but from the smoke billowing out of chimneys she knew there had to be NPCs about.

She heard the sound of splintering wood and turned to see Hollis smashing through the door of a house. Apparently the time for stealth had passed. She ran through the empty town square, back toward the others as Naveen and Shasta followed the diminutive Fighter into the building.

"What's he doing?" she shouted to Leo.

"Stopping the forges!" Leo shouted back, his eyes wild. Across the town square Carsten was breaking down the door of another house and charging inside with his mace raised high. Leo dashed off in that direction and Suzanne followed him, her uneasiness growing.

It would have been better if they had found a battalion inside. A squadron of guards, an armed resistance. But there was only a family of smiths—two parents and two children. They huddled against their forge, staring at the Pyxians and Suzanne with eyes full of fear.

Their stares hit Suzanne like an arrow. She was used to hate in the eyes of NPCs as she fought them, anger and rage befitting her role of enemy.

The smiths stared at her with quieter emotion. Fear.

They had not been lying in wait, swords drawn for a battle. They had been hiding from her and she had found them. They were afraid of what she might do. Looking at the Altairi family, clutching each other like a shield, she was afraid of what she could do to them.

"Step away from the forge," Leo commanded, his voice as sharp as the steel the Altairi forged. He pointed his heavy stave at the Altairi. Leo was a War Priest, a class that focused more on healing and support than fighting, but Suzanne had fought beside the prince enough to know he could do serious damage with his staff. The Altairi Citizens clung tighter together, but none of them moved.

"If you won't clear the way . . ." Leo menaced,

advancing. Suzanne reached out and grabbed his cloak. He whirled to face her.

"What are you doing?" he demanded.

"What are *you* doing?" she yelled back. "You're just going to cut them down?"

Leo hesitated. He looked like he finally understood that these Altairi were just Citizens.

"Please," she said. "Step aside. We're only here to destroy the forge. We don't want to hurt any of you."

A cry pierced the night, followed by a loud crash. Naveen, Shasta, and Hollis's work, most likely. Suzanne guessed they had favored a more direct approach.

The mother looked at Suzanne and gave a short nervous laugh. It was nearly a whimper. "Beg pardon," she said, "but I can't see how you mean that. You break the forge and how are we to earn a living? This is a town of smiths, miss, and we've got no way to feed our children should these fires go out."

"At least you'll have your children," Leo roared. The mother flinched away from him and clutched her son tighter.

Suzanne wanted to smack him. He was only making things worse.

"King Ramses himself ordered us to keep the forges hot, sir, day and night," the father begged. "If we don't give him the steel he needs then we won't be lasting long."

"You could run," Suzanne said.

"Where?" the man asked, laughing hollowly. "Ramses's reach is long and we are not classed like you. We won't last against the monsters on the road. We were dead soon as you showed up."

"Head to Zenith City," Suzanne suggested. "Hide among the refugees. Start a new life."

The NPC opened his mouth to argue again but a look from Leo quelled him. "She is offering you a chance," the prince snarled. "That is more than you would get from your king. Thank her and leave before her mercy dries up."

Still huddled together, the Altairi shuffled toward the door. Carsten stepped aside to let them pass. At the door of their house, the mother paused. "Thank you," she said to Suzanne. Her voice was hardly a whisper, drenched with venom.

"No," Suzanne replied. "I'm sorry."

The woman made a sound crossed between a sob and a laugh and left.

Carsten and Leo set to work destroying the forge. When the fires were gone and the forge nothing but dissipating pixels, Leo led the way out into the night. Suzanne looked around and saw several of the buildings were already collapsed by the other members of the party. She wanted to say something to Leo. She wanted to stop all of this. But he had already gone to join his friends. There were many more homes to destroy and many more refugees to make before they were through.

Chapter 5

"You defied me."

Libra's voice was dead calm. She looked at each member of the raiding party in turn, from Naveen to Carsten to Shasta to Hollis. Her gaze lingered on Leo long enough for the prince to look down in shame, and finally, the queen of Pyxis turned to regard Suzanne.

Suzanne heard no emotion in Libra's voice, just the fact of the matter. The queen ordered them not to go to Altair, not to raid the forges, and they did it anyway. All because Leo was convinced he was right.

Where was his surety now? Suzanne waited

for the prince to speak. He remained silent in his shame.

"My queen," Naveen said, gesturing to the other NPCs. "We did not know you had forbidden this. We assumed your brother spoke on your authority."

"So you claim exemption in your ignorance?"

The Piker stiffened. "No," he replied. "I just . . . "

His words trailed off, futile in the face of what he had done. Of what they had all done, together.

The town of Riversforge lay in ruins, its Citizens scattered as refugees throughout Altair, fugitives from the cruelty of their own king. Suzanne had stopped Leo from slaying any of the Altairi, but how long would they survive in the wild without their walls to protect them from the monsters of the realm?

Libra was waiting for them when they returned to camp, along with a squad of armed Pyxians. Suzanne didn't even have time to find Brit and

Mikayla and talk to them about what she had done. She wished her friends were with her now. She could stomach a lecture by herself, but the cold disappointment in Libra's voice was too much for her alone.

And she felt alone in Libra's great tent. Naveen and the others would not look at her or Leo, and Leo kept staring at the floor.

"You four are dismissed," Libra said. "I will send word later once I have decided what to do with you."

Led by Hollis, their four accomplices reiterated their apologies and shuffled out. Shasta was last to exit. The Monk shot an apologetic look back at Suzanne before leaving.

Once they were gone Libra turned back to Suzanne. "I had hoped you would influence my brother's decisions, not the other way around."

"It wasn't her fault," Leo said, speaking up at last. His voice quavered. "Suzanne was against it. She . . . she protected the Citizens."

"Protected them?" Libra's voice shook with disbelief. "How? By destroying their homes? By turning their king against them?"

"You speak as if Ramses is not our enemy," Leo replied.

"And you act as if hurting your enemies is all that matters," the queen replied.

Suzanne couldn't stay silent any longer. "I screwed up, okay?" She shook her head. "We all screwed up. We should have listened to you."

"You should have," Libra said.

"But Leo wasn't wrong," Suzanne continued, her voice gaining strength as she spoke. "We weren't wrong to cripple the Altairi Army. But we were wrong to just leave those refugees. They're our responsibility and we should have taken care of them."

"You would have killed them?" the queen interjected incredulously.

"No. We should have brought them back to camp with us. Rigel can always use more hands in the forge. You didn't see them. They were working for Ramses because they were afraid, not because they were loyal. We could have helped them. We could have freed them."

She stared defiantly at Libra. Of course she felt responsible. She felt responsible for every NPC in Io, every artificial intelligence she had created. Suzanne didn't think it mattered why she felt responsible. She knew she could never explain herself entirely to Libra, never share the truth of where she and her friends really came from and what Io really was. But that didn't matter. Even if this world was designed as a game, Suzanne wasn't playing a game now. She meant every word she had said and she hoped the queen understood that.

Libra was silent for several minutes after Suzanne spoke. When she finally spoke, her voice was softer, free of her earlier disappointment.

"Would you excuse us, Suzanne? I would speak to my brother alone."

Suzanne nodded, but she was worried she had

gone too far, said something that she couldn't take back. And what were they going to talk about that she couldn't be here to hear it?

Leo smiled and gave her hand a reassuring squeeze. "I'll find you after we're done," he said.

The glare from the sun hit Suzanne right in the eyes as she exited Libra's tent. It was near midday; when she entered, it had been morning. She took a deep breath to calm herself and felt two hands shove her hard in the back. Stumbling to regain her balance she looked around for who had pushed her. It was Brit.

"You dumbass," Brit said. "I can't believe you went to Altair without us."

Mikayla stood beside Brit, her arms crossed in disapproval. "You didn't really follow through with Leo's plan?" she asked.

Suzanne didn't feel the need to answer that rhetorical question.

"Of course she did," Brit answered for her. Affecting a high voice of mockery she spoke in teasing, "Let's go kill Citizens, Leo. We can make out while we stab them."

"Shut up," Suzanne said. She wasn't in the mood for Brit's shit, not today. Brit stopped the teasing immediately, which was a pleasant surprise. Suzanne realized she had her don't-fuck-with-me face on. What she really wanted was to be alone for a while, maybe bury her head in a pillow and scream out her frustration.

But her friends wouldn't leave her alone. Brit and Mikayla fell into step as she walked away from Libra's tent.

"Did Libra say anything about your punishment?" Mikayla asked with concern. "We went looking for you last night, but we couldn't find you. I figured you'd gone off somewhere with Leo but then we heard a bunch of other NPCs were missing."

Brit picked up the story from there. "Libra was furious. I'd never seen her so mad before. It was scary."

Suzanne stopped walking and turned to face Brit. If Libra had scared Brit, then she must be truly frightening when angry. Were her friends mad at her? No, that wasn't it. They were worried about her, worried she was in over her head.

They went back to their tent where Suzanne explained that she had gotten in over her head, but not dangerously. She told them everything, from the stealth crawl through the woods to the last collapsed building in Riversforge.

Mikayla shuddered. "It must have felt awful," she said.

"Yeah," Suzanne said. "It kind of did."

She was sitting on her bed while Brit and Mikayla sat on Brit's bed opposite. When Suzanne told them about that first family of smiths, Mikayla scowled and Brit looked away into the distance. Now Brit spoke up.

"The whole thing's fucked," she said. "I mean, how were you supposed to know they were families?

Why couldn't you have made this game with actual bad guys instead of all these Citizens?"

"What do you call Ramses?" Suzanne asked.

Brit was happy to call Ramses many things. When she was done, and Mikayla and Suzanne had stopped laughing, Mikayla said, "You were right, though. I bet you most of those refugees would be happy being on our side of the war."

The fact that her friends had her back cheered Suzanne. She heard footsteps approaching. "Can I come in?" Leo called from outside the tent.

Brit made a face and Mikayla punched her in the arm. Suzanne called back, "Sure," still laughing.

Leo stuck his head through the flaps. "Libra asked me to send you back to her."

"Are you in trouble?" Suzanne asked.

He shrugged. "We're at war with a mad king. I'd say we're all in trouble."

"That's not what I meant."

"I know. I've been demoted. And I'll be demoted more if you don't hurry up and get back to Libra."

Demoted? What did that even mean? But Leo would say nothing more as he led her back toward the center of the camp. She could hear Rigel's smiths hammering in the distance and the sounds of other NPCs sparring and training.

When she entered Libra's tent again she found the queen seated at the council table, studying a map of the Ion River. Suzanne cleared her throat and Libra looked up, beckoning her to have a seat at the table. The queen didn't look angry, Suzanne thought, but she could feel her stomach doing backflips from apprehension.

"If I were a different queen, I would have your head for speaking to me as you have."

"If you were a different queen you would have thrown me in chains as soon as you met me and my friends."

Libra's mouth cracked into a smile. "Fair enough. To be frank, you have placed me in a difficult position. You disobeyed my order. If you were a Pyxian I would dismiss you from my army and be done with it. Yet you are not a Pyxian. You fight alongside us because you choose to, not out of obligation to your home."

"I cannot allow for insubordination," the queen continued. "So you must be punished. From now on, all your free time must go to helping Rigel in his forge."

Suzanne wasn't sure she had heard Libra correctly. That was hardly any punishment at all as Suzanne was spending most of her free time helping Rigel anyway. Libra looked at her expectantly.

"Thanks," Suzanne managed, "but what about your brother?"

The queen smiled. "As for Leo . . . he will lead the first party into Altair, with the intention of providing passage for any refugees who wish to defect. Doubtless many will not trust us, but there will be those we can help."

Is that what Leo meant by demoted? Suzanne

wondered why he had used that word. Still, that was hardly a punishment either, more of a compromise between the queen's plan and Leo's.

"Now be off," Libra said. "As you said, Rigel always needs help with the forge, and until my brother brings back those smiths from Altair, he'll have to settle for you."

Suzanne thanked the queen again and ran toward the sounds of pounding metal. It was only when she reached the forge that she realized the unease she'd been feeling since her trip to Altair had disappeared.

Chapter 6

Brit wasn't going to wait much longer. Sailing down the Ion River to the village Fen's End took them all of the morning, and Lynx said that sailing back up would take even longer. That wasn't even accounting for the fact that they had to ferry all the willing villagers across the river to Pyxis, which could take hours, depending on how much the NPCs insisted on taking with them. This was Brit's third time going out on these "rescue missions," as Suzanne called them. But Brit knew what they really were: escort missions, and there's no worse kind of mission than a fucking escort mission. If she wanted to make it back to the Pyxian camp before the week ended, then she couldn't spend all day listening to this old NPC bluster.

"We can't trust them is what I'm saying," the old NPC bleated. He was Brit's least favorite kind of NPC, the kind that loved to hear themselves talk. For the umpteenth time she wondered why Suze couldn't have made the game with a way to skip dialogue.

Getting to Fen's Edge had taken a while but the trip down was without incident. Right when dawn cracked they'd gotten in the boat, her and Mikayla. Lynx held the rudder and carried in her inventory the official offer of friendship from Libra to these villagers. Brit and Mikayla had been sent along in case Lynx ran into any trouble.

The current carried them south at a lazy pace, the waters of the Ion River a clear blue until they reached the Fenlands. Fen's Edge lived up to its name, sitting on the border of that great swamp that swallowed the southernmost part of Altair.

And it was truly a swamp. When Lynx steered the boat in for docking, Mikayla hopped onto the shore to tie it down. Brit watched her sink in the soft peat up to her ankles. That was gross, but hiking through the fens proved even grosser. The ground sucked at their feet with every step and long vines hung like curtains in their way. Twice the trees grew so close together that Brit couldn't pass through. The first time they looked for another way around. The second time Brit took out her halberd and got to chopping.

Trees, vines, and swamp gunk didn't earn her any experience points. There were few monsters in the swamp, mostly bat-like screechers and the odd weremonkey. Screechers flew and weremonkeys swung from vines, both out of her range. The creatures were all so low-leveled that they wouldn't attack of their own volition. So bushwhacking was made all the better by the soundtrack of hooting and screeching.

Brit was at level eighteen, two levels away from

the magical twenty. Suze told her that's when she'd change into an advanced class, powering up pretty much everything. There were a couple paths a Fighter could take, but Brit just wanted one that was badass. And maybe one that could kill a screecher.

Finally, they'd found Fen's Edge. The entire village rested on planks lashed together like a raft. Like a raft, if enough of the villagers gathered on one side, all of Fen's Edge would tilt in that direction. There wasn't even a garrison for Ramses's army, so there wouldn't be any fighting. *What a shitty village*, Brit thought, her mood completely sour. She couldn't imagine why anyone, human or NPC, would want to stay long.

But the NPCs felt differently. As soon as Lynx finished reading the letter from Libra, the villagers of Fen's Edge began to argue. To begin with, half of them didn't trust Pyxians at all. They fully bought into the rumors and legends they'd heard about the other kingdom. So then Lynx and

Mikayla had to address each of their concerns, one at a time.

Lynx promised that, A) they weren't here to steal anyone's children, B) they weren't going to take anyone out in the river and drown them halfway across, and C) that there wasn't a legion of Pyxians waiting on the other shore to do child stealing or murdering. Even then, none of the Altairi made any sign of wanting to go.

"Can't we just head back? We'll tell Libra that we tried," Brit muttered to Mikayla.

Mikayla looked up at her with that typical Mikayla face, doe-eyed with concern for the poor villagers. "We've got to wreck their forges and we can't just leave them here! Ramses will send someone to kill them if they don't make their quotas," Mikayla insisted, as if Brit hadn't heard that explanation a thousand times. The best and worst thing about being friends with Mikayla was that you could always count on her to do the right thing.

Brit sighed. Of all the parts of being stuck in a video game, this was her least favorite. If she was just playing on a screen she could tune out through the negotiations, spamming the button to advance dialogue. But as long as she was stuck in Io, she was stuck listening to the complaints of every single NPC.

"No, we want to set you up in a Pyxian village," Lynx said. The princess was doing her best to stay calm, but she was clearly running out of patience. She was more like her brother Leo than she initially let on. The villagers argued back and Brit could see their rescue mission was on the verge of becoming a skirmish.

Mikayla stepped in, ready as ever to smooth things over. "There's an empty Pyxian village right across the river," she explained. "The land there is much better. You won't have to live on this raft and there's a ton of ore for your forges. No one's going to set a quota or your prices."

"If your Pyxian village is so great then how come it's got no one in it?" the ornery old NPC asked.

Lynx's eyes blazed with anger. "Ramses's army killed all the Citizens."

That hushed most of the villagers. Unfortunately, not the old goat. "Then you are leading us to get killed, I knew it!" he shouted.

"Look," Brit said, unable to listen to him anymore. "There aren't any soldiers in that part of Pyxis anymore because we drove them out. We're giving you a choice between working yourselves to death in a shithole for an asshole or living in a nice place doing whatever the hell you want." She checked herself before she mentioned they'd be wrecking Fen's Edge's forges anyway. Past experience told her to keep that on the down low.

The villagers turned and talked it over with each other. It looked like some of them were changing their minds, but Brit wasn't going to get her hopes up. For all she knew they'd be talking it over until tomorrow.

"What's all this then?" a voice roared. Brit saw him coming over the heads of the villagers, a Defender with an auburn mustache nearly as large as his shields. He was big—bigger than her character. Stamped on both shields he carried and the breastplate of his armor was the four-pillared insignia of Altair.

"Sir Errol," the old NPC squeaked, suddenly supplicant in the face of the mustached soldier. "They were going to steal our children and murder us, they were. They're a bunch of evil Pyxians."

"Hmm? Pyxians?" Whenever Errol spoke his mustache fluttered. The Defender stared at Brit and the others, clearly unimpressed.

"You're a liar, Old Ogden," a woman shouted. She'd been one of the one's afraid of child stealing. Brit was surprised to hear her speak out now. "These three offered us a better life in Pyxis, said we don't have to work for Ramses no more. Said we could sell our own wares and do whatever we wanted without fear of you disappearing us."

Other villagers stood behind her, nodding stubbornly. "That's right!" another villager shouted, pointing at Brit. "She says we won't have to worry about falling in the fens or getting eat by a shadowcat no more. She says we're gonna live on grass and ground."

Errol's head swiveled toward the villager who ducked behind another NPC to hide. "You are all Citizens of Altair," Errol drawled. "Without your efforts, there could be no glorious war."

"Glorious butchering, more like," Lynx spat at him. Brit nodded. She might not have a bleeding heart like Mikayla, but she was sick to death of Altairi bullshit.

"Oh ho. Little Pyxian. You will not taint these poor souls with your lies." Errol took a step toward Lynx and the raft carrying the village shuddered. "You are far from your home and under arrest for crimes against the crown."

"Why don't you let them choose where they want to go instead of keeping them here like prisoners?" Mikayla said. Her hand was on the hilt of her estoc.

The Defender guffawed. "What is this nonsense? They are citizens of the greatest kingdom ever known, the flock of the great king Ramses. To serve a man such as him is an honor. We trust in the judgment of his wisdom."

"And besides," he added, his mustache trembling with menace, "any who go with these three is a traitor to the crown and an enemy to the people and will be dealt with as such." He smashed the two huge shields he carried together; the sound rang throughout the swamp.

"Just shut the fuck up already!" Brit shouted. "Look, clearly none of them want to be here. So how about this? If you love this place so much you stay here and the rest of us will go somewhere nice, okay?"

Errol bellowed another laugh. "You will make a fine example for the more rebellious among these Citizens. Will all three of you attack me at once, like the cravens you are, or shall we settle this like men?"

Brit looked at Lynx and Mikayla. Mikayla gestured for her to go ahead.

"Oh thank god," Brit said, grabbing her halberd out of her inventory. "I've been dying to hit somebody all day. I'll take you on."

That seemed to amuse Errol even more. "Well said. It seems you Pyxians are not short on courage. If I defeat you, your friends may submit to my mercy. No need to ruin three pretty faces."

"I'm not a Pyxian. I was actually on your side until me and my friends figured out that Ramses is a dick," Brit said.

"You'll pay for defaming the king," the Defender promised.

"Whatever," Brit said. "If I win, you have to shut up and shave your mustache.

The villagers stepped back, forming a ring around the two of them. A few cheered her on, but most watched, silent with anxiety. *They're probably worried about what's going to happen if I lose*, Brit thought. As always, she ignored her own nerves.

"Are you sure you can handle this?" Lynx asked her. The princess eyed the Defender uncertainly.

"Please," Mikayla answered for Brit. "She's got this."

Hearing that was all the encouragement Brit needed. Mikayla stood on tiptoe to whisper in her ear. "Don't kill him. We don't want to scare the villagers."

Brit rolled her eyes. Since Errol hadn't initiated a duel, she would only get experience points if she killed him. She rolled back her shoulders, loosening her limbs for combat. Not that it mattered, but the ritual centered Brit. She lowered her halberd and waited for Errol to charge.

Errol jumped. As his bulky frame came crashing down, his side of Fen's Edge dipped under the swamp. The whole village tilted toward him, sending the villagers stumbling. Brit suddenly found herself standing on a slope, slipping downhill right at the Defender's shields.

He jabbed forward with his right as Brit found her footing and pivoted left around him. She took a two-handed swing at his back. Errol's other shield was there, and her weapon glanced harmlessly off.

Errol threw himself up again, and again the village tilted as he landed. This time Brit had to throw herself into a roll to get out of the way of his attack. She got back up as quickly as she could, but Errol was already on her. He pounced forward with his shields, throwing them at her like punches. Brit raised her halberd to defend herself, yet with the raft still rocking she couldn't find good footing and found herself giving up ground with every block.

She saw her opening when the Defender jabbed with his left. She spun her halberd upward, hacking at his armpit. The Defender howled and dropped his left shield. But that left Brit unable to block the right, which smashed her off her feet.

She landed in a heap on her shoulders. Her eyes flicked up to her health bar. She wasn't in the red yet, but that one hit had knocked off a sizable chunk of her health. Better to finish this fast.

Errol flexed out his left arm, testing it. He stooped and grabbed the shield he dropped and jumped up again. This time Brit was ready for him. She chopped overhand, not at Errol, but at where he would land. The wood of the raft splintered, and when the Defender landed, it cracked and he fell through. He sank into the bog up to his armpits and stuck. Brit watched him wriggle for a minute, but it was clear he wasn't able to get himself free.

Most of the villagers broke out into a ragged cheer. Old Ogden grumbled something about them all being doomed, but Brit was beyond caring. Mikayla ran up and hugged her and Lynx clapped her on the back.

"Craven!" Errol shouted, still struggling. "A coward's trick! Free me and let us finish this."

"I intend to," Brit said, walking toward him, her halberd slung over her shoulder.

"Hey!" Mikayla shouted, but Brit ignored her and kept walking.

She knelt by the trapped Defender. To his credit, he didn't flinch away. Brit sighed, louder than ever, and stuck her halberd back in her inventory. Taking out a knife she slashed at his head. The villagers let out a gasp of horror.

"How dare you!" Errol shouted. Brit stood up and laughed, holding his mustache in her hands. Mikayla and Lynx joined in, and everyone except for Errol and Old Ogden was laughing by the time the mustache turned into pixels and was gone.

"Who's ready to go to Pyxis?" Brit asked and the villagers cheered again.

"I ain't going," Old Ogden said. He crossed his arms and stomped his foot, but none of the villagers could reason with him.

Exasperated, Brit turned to Mikayla, hoping she could convince the old coot. Mikayla was pointing at the hole Errol was stuck in. "The swamp's coming up through it."

Brit looked where she pointed and saw the gunk of the fen bubbling up onto the raft. Soon the villagers noticed, making them move that much faster to get off the raft and onto firmer ground. Soon they were all following Lynx back toward the river.

By then the raft was really sinking. "Nice," Brit said. "Saves us the hassle of wrecking the place."

Mikayla nodded. "But what are we going to do about him?"

While the other villagers had grabbed their belongings—smiths their tools, merchants their stores, and so on—Ogden had stayed where he was, refusing the cajoling of his fellow villagers.

Brit walked over to him. "You leave me be," he said, his voice panicky. "I'm not going to fight you so you're nothing more than a bully if you beat me up."

She did not deign to reply. Scooping the old

NPC up, she carried him in her arms like a baby back to the river, leaving the sinking town and the stuck Defender to the swamp.

Then there was the whole hassle of ferrying the Altairi across the river to Pyxis, which took more trips than Brit would've imagined. Finally, they were done and could begin the arduous row back up the Ion River to the main Pyxian camp.

It was only when they finally made it back to shore the next day that Brit noticed her experience points had gone up. But she hadn't killed Errol or anything else, so that shouldn't have happened. She lay down on her cot, resigned to ask Suze about it tomorrow. And mingled in her pre-sleep thoughts was the promise of changing her class soon.

Chapter 7

The forge spot appeared right at the neck of the armor. Suzanne brought down one hammer and then the other. If she hit the armor just right, instead of the normal clang she'd hear a chime. That signaled a critical forge. She'd been on a bit of a hot streak—each of her strikes set the armor chiming. Suzanne grinned with satisfaction as the last forge spot disappeared.

Rigel walked over to examine her handicraft. "Fine work," he said. That was as good praise as she was going to get from the forge master. Rigel wasn't one to dally over compliments. "Hollis," he snapped. "Flame's getting low. Go stoke it back up."

Hollis ran to attend to the forge. Suzanne noticed that ever since their mission to Altair, Hollis was bending over backwards to stay on Rigel's good side. But that wasn't the only reason she was watching Hollis. She was always trying to learn more about how things worked in Io. After a week working for Rigel full time she had the forging process down. Scrapping forges in Altair gave her a better idea of how they were constructed, but she knew she was missing some crucial element of how they operated. Hollis emerged from the supply tent with an armful of resplendent crystals.

Energite. That was what Suzanne had missed, what made the forge fires burn. Hollis stooped next to the dwindling forge and opened a compartment at its base. He placed the crystals delicately inside and then shut the compartment again. Curiously, the flames rose higher even though Hollis hadn't stoked them all. Suzanne was about to ask Hollis to explain what he had done when Rigel shouted for the young Fighter again, sending him off to deliver the newly forged goods. As a result, Suzanne was left alone with her forge and her curiosity.

Well, Suzanne wasn't the kind of girl who'd sit still with her curiosity. More than once during her childhood her dad found her sitting with a piece of disassembled hardware in front of her. The toaster had been easy enough for her to put back together, but she'd needed her dad's help when she messed with their monitor.

In that spirit she felt around the base of her anvil, as Hollis had done. She had never noticed that compartment before. It wasn't visible, but she felt a switch click and the little door swung open.

The Energite was nested in the compartment. As Suzanne watched, the crystals lost their luster and faded. Once their color was dun, they crumbled into pixels which melded with the sides of the compartment.

She would have never guessed that the NPCs

were using Energite to make items. *But how did you think they made them?* With a chuckle she realized she simply hadn't thought about that. Suzanne's crafting system made it so that once a character got enough ore, they could try to forge an item. Their skill would determine their success. The NPCs had taken her basic design and improved it with Energite.

"Don't go messing with that!" Rigel's voice was sharp behind her. Suzanne closed the compartment and stood to face the smith.

"I'm sorry," she said. "I was just curious."

"Curious is fine. Meddling's what I'm worried about." Suzanne promised she wouldn't fiddle with the forges and she'd focus on fixing the gear. Only when he heard her hammer ringing did the smith leave her alone to do her work and think.

She thought back to the castle in Zenith City, the capital of Altair. There were doors and elevators there that were powered by Energite, and she hadn't designed those either. At the time she had been too overwhelmed by being at court to question anybody about it, and she never got a chance to examine the mechanisms herself. Now she would have given anything just to understand how it all worked. None of it made sense to her, but she knew she was still thinking in real-world terms. In Io, you could put Energite in an anvil and an unconnected fire would rise higher. *Not unconnected*, she corrected herself. *You just don't know how it works yet.* It was crazy to think how much the NPCs had deduced about their own world. Suzanne realized it wasn't that different from scientists back in her own world. Why wasn't there a Wikipedia for Io where she could look up the history of forging?

She turned over the gauntlet that she was working on and struck the new forge spot that appeared. Thinking back on designing the game was like remembering a different life. She finished the gauntlets and handed them to one of the new NPCs at camp, an Altairi who had come back with

Brit and Mikayla. They tried to find a place in Pyxian villages for all of the Altairi they helped cross the river, but invariably some ended up at the main camp, eager to be useful in any way they could. This particular NPC, a girl who looked to be about Suzanne's age, was taking the finished items to be redistributed among the army. Another new Pyxian handed Suzanne a set of knee-high greaves, the next item that needed repairing.

Looking up, Suzanne saw that Lynx was watching her. Suzanne set down her hammers and waved as Lynx walked over. She hadn't interacted with the princess that much, but Lynx was always at the council meetings and Suzanne knew she'd been going on missions with Brit and Mikayla. Still, if Lynx was coming to find her that could mean only one thing: Libra was summoning Suzanne.

"So how are the rescues going?" Suzanne asked as the two of them made their way to the center of camp. "I haven't seen Brit or Mikayla at all this past week."

"We've been busy," Lynx replied. "We have been to most of the southern villages along the river. So far the villagers have all crossed over. Word is spreading. The last few we came to, the villagers were expecting us."

"In a good way?"

"Sometimes. At Numrich, the villagers had already packed their belongings and were ready to go before we got there."

"And the others?"

Lynx laughed. "There were soldiers waiting for us at Crescent Point. It was a good thing we had Mikayla with us; she spotted them before they spotted us. I don't think we could have avoided a fight otherwise. But when we came back to Crescent Point, the soldiers were gone and the villagers were all too eager to cross over to our side. I don't think these Altairi have a great love for the army of Ramses."

Suzanne knew as much from her own experience talking to Altairi Citizens.

"But how goes your own mission?" Lynx asked.

"What mission? You mean the forges? Rigel has us working hard, but that's only because there's so much left to do."

"I speak of a different flame," Lynx said, a mischievous glint in her eye. "My brother."

Suzanne blushed. It was one thing to endure teasing from Brit and Mikayla and an entirely different matter to talk about Leo with his sister.

"It's going . . . great," she offered as Lynx laughed again.

"I would hope so. Hearing Leo talk, I'm surprised the two of you manage to spend any time apart."

That didn't sound quite right to Suzanne. "What do you mean?" she asked.

"No need to look offended, I assure you. Just that my brother rarely commits to anything halfway. He tends to jump in feet first."

That sounded like Leo. The day before, Rigel had told her he had more helpers at the forge than he knew what to do with, so he gave her the day off. "Make sure the queen doesn't see," he warned her. "You're supposed to be serving out your punishment still."

Suzanne had found Leo sparring with Naveen in the training grounds. The two of them had wandered off together, losing themselves in the countryside of Pyxis. West of the camp the landscape broke into the rolling hills that dominated the kingdom and they spent the day talking and hiking, breaking only to deal with the odd monster dumb enough to challenge them, and for a picnic.

Suzanne had worried that she was being clichéd, but the notion of a picnic was completely novel to the Pyxian prince. When she withdrew the food from her inventory—fruits like apples but with a peel, and a hard loaf of bread—Leo asked her what she intended to do with it.

"Eat it, dummy," she replied, biting into the fruit. The NPCs ate sparingly, only when their hunger demanded it. If they didn't eat every few days they would lose health, but that was as far as their appetites went. There wasn't a single gourmand in the entire world of Io. The idea of a meal as an activity was as foreign to the NPCs as the idea of a car or an airplane.

The same restrictions went for Suzanne and her friends. The taste of the food was inconsistent, which she assumed was due to how the TII interacted with her sense of taste. But these apple-like fruits were almost always good, and the bread, if nothing else, had the same fortifying texture of an actual loaf.

Thinking back, Suzanne could hardly remember a word of their conversation. What she could remember was the feeling of being with him, lying side-by-side in the grass as they watched the clouds in the sky. The hills were lousy with razorbacks—massive boars with metal tusks—but the monsters trundled past without bothering the two of them. It was as if the whole world of Io was at peace while they were together.

He asked her, "Do you miss your home?" That was after they had the picnic, after they had spent the day laughing and talking and just being alone together, while they walked back toward the Pyxian camp with the sun setting behind them.

She paused before answering, but came up with the truth anyway. "Yes," she said. When he didn't ask anything else, she reached out and held his hand. "But sometimes I miss it less."

The setting sun caught in his hair, crowning him with a blazing mane. She placed a hand on the back of his neck and pulled him into a kiss. When she held him, when he held her, it was all true. She missed home less. All her other thoughts were buried beneath the moment. He kissed her again and broke away. The moment ended and the kiss became as much a memory as her home. As much a memory as reality.

"It's going great," she repeated to Lynx, more confident, more sure. Because her relationship was going great. Suzanne had decided to let what happened in Riverforge stay in Riverforge. The princess didn't push her to answer any more questions. They walked the rest of the way to Libra's in silence.

Leo was waiting at the council table when they got there, along with Brit and Mikayla and Mallon and the queen herself. Rigel was still at the forge. In his spot sat a stranger.

Even with his back turned to her, Suzanne could tell that this NPC was no Pyxian. He wore the bulky armor of an Altairi, the same bulky armor she herself wore. Draped over the NPC's armor was a blood-red cape. Suzanne took her seat next to Leo and saw, stamped on the breastplate of NPC's armor were the four crimson pillars carrying an orb, the insignia of Ramses.

Chapter 8

"Lynx, Suzanne, I present to you Dante, King Ramses's envoy." Libra gestured to the Altairi garbed in armor. He was a serious-looking NPC—long frown lines were etched around his mouth. He regarded the assembled counsel with a look crossed between disdain and distrust. Wherever his gaze fell, it was met with an equally hostile stare. From the two-handed long sword strapped to his back, Suzanne guessed he was a Paladin.

"Dante has brought a message from the king concerning the war," Libra continued, ignoring the staring match going on around her council table. "I asked him to wait on delivering it until we were all present. Dante, if you would please say your piece now."

"It is peace I come to speak of," Dante replied. "Peace and justice for the peoples of Altair and Pyxis."

"Yes, for both kingdoms," he insisted, responding to the skeptical look on the Pyxians' faces. "For great King Ramses, in his infinite compassion, has sought to restore order not only to his own land but to yours as well."

Leo opened his mouth to interrupt, but Libra spoke up before he could. "That is good to hear. I am sure we all desire peace. Please, Dante, continue." She gave her brother a look that Suzanne could read clear as day: shut up and wait until the envoy has had his say.

The envoy paused for a second to gather his thoughts before resuming his speech. "Peace is the great king's first concern. He offers to withdraw his troops—the guarantors of Altairi freedom—from

Pyxis should certain conditions be met. First, you must guarantee the removal of all Pyxian raiders from Altair. Second, all hostages captured in your raids on Altairi villages must be returned to their sovereign soil."

"What hostages?" Lynx asked. "You mean the Citizens who willingly followed us to Pyxis?"

If Dante heard her words he made no sign of it. He was so good at maintaining his scowl that Suzanne wondered if the NPC could register any other emotion. Libra turned to caution Lynx toward silence, but the princess was satisfied with her question and smiled sweetly as her sister shot her an angry look. Libra asked the envoy's pardon and begged for him to resume.

"Where was I? Yes, peace. The great King Ramses asks that you free your hostages, recall your raiders, and he will likewise remove his peacekeepers from your lands. As a sign of good faith, he has already recalled half of his garrison stationed north of this camp."

Libra looked to Mallon, who headed the scouting operations for the NPCs. Mallon gave a curt nod. Only the day before she had reported something similar, although by her estimate under a third, and certainly not half of the Altairi had crossed back to their own land. Suzanne had concluded, with the others, that Ramses was recalling troops to protect his forges from the so-called raiders. But maybe he really did intend to make peace.

Still, Suzanne knew better than to trust the king. She still remembered Ramses promising to help her, Mikayla, and Brit. Yet instead of helping them, Ramses sent his troops to kill them, then framed them for murder and tried to have them imprisoned.

Dante cleared his throat and continued his speech. "The foundation of this peace will be justice. The king understands that because of this war, the capital of Pyxis has been destroyed. Yet buildings can hardly be blamed for this misunderstanding between our kingdoms. King Ramses will send over a new force, an army of smiths and masons, builders, and laborers to repair your capital and restore the seat of Pyxian power."

Across the table, Suzanne watched Brit roll her eyes. Suzanne knew what that meant: no way Ramses was going to help rebuild Pyxis out of the goodness of his heart. The question was what he wanted in return.

Dante answered that question when he stared at Suzanne. "Justice upheld by only one side is no justice," the Paladin proclaimed. "And as King Ramses is just, so too must you be, Libra, queen of the Pyxians." Even though he spoke to Libra, his eyes never left Suzanne. "So for justice and to ensure future friendship between our lands, Ramses asks that you extradite the criminals known as Brit, Mikayla, and Suzanne. They have crimes in Altair to answer for."

Multiple people spoke at once. Leo shouted, "Absolutely not," Mikayla said, "You have to be kidding me," Lynx just laughed, and Brit asked, "What does extradite mean?"

"It means hand us over to the great King Ramses," Suzanne answered her. She didn't realize Ramses wanted them badly enough to go to all the trouble of ending a war and rebuilding the Pyxian capital.

Brit joined the rest of them in scowling, but Libra simply said, her voice as polite as ever, "Apologies for the interruption. Is there anything else to the king's terms?"

Dante blinked, as if taken aback by Libra's courtesy. "Those are his terms—peace and justice. If these terms are unacceptable, we will turn to the old ways."

The old ways? Suzanne wondered what that could possibly mean.

"Thank you," Libra said. "We must now discuss the terms amongst ourselves. Brit, please take Dante to your tent so he may rest and refresh himself while we talk. You will find Naveen there.

Remind him that Dante is my personal guest and that no one may harm him."

"Whatever," Brit said. Standing, she towered over the Paladin, but if Dante was intimidated he didn't show it. He followed Brit out of the tent.

Once he was gone Leo spoke up at once. "You cannot seriously be considering these terms."

"Of course not," Libra smiled. "But I wonder if you listened to them as I did, brother. Ramses wants us to end our raids, as he calls them. Undoubtedly that means they are having their desired effect. He offers to help us rebuild our Capital, which would move the main bulk of our forces away from the river and give him intimate knowledge of the Capital's defense."

Mallon nodded. "It's easy to see what he has to gain from all this. And if he isn't winning this war, it makes sense for him to try to get out and save as much face as he can."

"We should propose our own peace," Lynx said.

"Tell him if he pulls his troops out, we will do the same."

Brit returned while they were discussing how to phrase their terms. "So I take it we aren't going back to prison?" she asked. When the answer was a resounding *no*, Brit said, "Good, I really wasn't trying to beat up the entire Pyxian royal family."

Everyone laughed, but something was bothering Suzanne. Wasn't Ramses just going to reject their terms as they had rejected his? The King had wanted his Citizens back as well as the girls, and there was no way he was going to settle for getting neither. She told her concerns to the rest of the table.

"I fear you are correct." Libra looked solemn. "I wish to end this war so we may begin to rebuild Pyxis. More than anything else, that is my wish. But if we go back on our word and turn those Citizens over to Ramses, or if we give him the three of you, then we will be liars and not worthy of the peace we have earned. Ritual combat is the only solution."

"It's the old way," Leo explained. "Back before there were the two kingdoms, each town and village was its own ruler. Whenever a disagreement rose up between two, they would settle the matter with a trial of combat. Whoever won the trial was judged to be in the right."

So that was the old way. True, she did design combat before any other part of Io, but at that point the program barely resembled this world. There was never a point in her development where every town ruled itself, she was sure of that. What Leo was describing sounded like something out of Arthurian legend. Back when the game was only combat, none of these NPCs existed. But the rest of the NPCs nodded along, as if they were all familiar with the idea of a trial by combat. She chalked it up to a quirk of the AI, a myth the NPCs developed to explain their world.

"Sounds like the way to do it," Brit said.

"Sure, maybe if you're strong. But would Ramses be down for that?" Mikayla asked. "He seems pretty set on getting everything he wants."

"He'd get it, if he wins." Mallon's voice was somber. "Winner takes all, that's the justice of ritual combat. Are you really so sure that we could beat whoever he throws at us?"

No one spoke. Suzanne knew they were all imagining the same thing: what would happen if Ramses won? Suzanne and Mikayla exchanged a look. Losing meant getting locked in Ramses's prison while their bodies slowly wasted away in the real world. It meant never going home again.

"Yes." Libra's voice was quiet but firm. "We will win because we must win. I am tired and our people are exhausted. We have no right to allow this war to continue longer than necessary. For our people, we must accept Ramses's offer and for our people we must win."

Mallon went to fetch Dante. She came back with the Paladin in tow. Libra stated the Pyxians' terms for peace, which the envoy rejected instantly, as they knew he would.

"You make a grave mistake," Dante cautioned. "Ramses offered terms for peace and justice and you have spurned them. Now nothing shall protect you from his wrath."

"Our strength will protect us," Leo replied coolly, "As it has before."

"Tell Ramses we await word of his terms for combat," Libra added.

"King Ramses," Dante corrected her.

"No. When we were talking of peace Ramses was a king. But now we talk of conflict and he is but an enemy." The edge crept back into Libra's voice. Suzanne remembered watching the queen crush an enemy in battle; she had a similar manner as she rose and ushered the Altairi envoy out.

The meeting was adjourned. Suzanne met up with Brit and Mikayla, and the three of them walked south out of the camp. Away from the

NPCs, they could talk freely without fear of anyone overhearing. Sometimes Suzanne wondered what would happen if an NPC found out that Io was all a game, and that Suzanne herself had designed it. Would they even believe what they heard? But right now there were more important things to think about.

They walked into the forest until they couldn't see the edge of the trees. Mikayla climbed up on the lower branches of a tall pine and took a seat on the crisscrossing branches. "Sometimes it feels less like we're stuck in a game and more like we're stuck in a movie," she said. "Like we don't even know who Ramses is going to throw at us, and now, if the Pyxians lose, we're fucked."

"So we'll beat them." Suzanne wished she were as confident as Brit sounded.

Mikayla also sounded unconvinced. "What if we don't get to fight? Then we're risking everything on a bunch of NPCs."

"Not just any NPCs," Suzanne said. "I'm pretty

sure I'd pick Libra to fight for me if I could pick anyone."

"Not Leo?" Brit asked. But she dropped the joke immediately. "Look, why don't we just ask Libra to let us fight? We're tougher than almost everyone here. And last time I checked, we've kicked the ass of every Altairi we've fought."

Suzanne remembered Brit's story about Errol, the Defender Brit had beat in the swamp. *We can win*, she told herself. But it didn't matter how many times she repeated those words. All she had to do was take a look at Mikayla fretting away and she would feel the uncertainty gnawing at her.

Chapter 9

"Who are we?"

"Pyxian!"

"Who are we?"

"Pyxian!"

Even standing behind the crowd, their answer was deafening. Libra repeated her question a third time, and a third time every NPC of the camp roared in response, "Pyxian!"

Brit sat on top of a supply cart, watching the spectacle. For good on two hours, the Pyxians chanted and cheered for themselves and their nation.

"It's like they're praying," Mikayla said.

Brit nodded. She didn't have another word for it.

On her left, Mikayla watched the end of the ceremony intently, but with nowhere near the intensity of Suzanne. Suzanne kept leaning forward to get a better look; Brit was afraid her friend was going to fall off the supply cart.

For once, Brit didn't think Suzanne was weird for geeking out over Io. They'd spent weeks of game-time in this camp, and Brit didn't recognize half the NPCs assembled. Where had they all come from? She knew Mallon's scouts had come back from the field, and most of the River Guard had joined back up, but that didn't account for the sheer numbers in this crowd, and it certainly didn't explain where all these Citizens had come from.

Some came as converts from Altair, Brit knew. She had helped some of them cross the river herself. But the others must have been in the camp the whole time. Sometimes Io felt small to Brit, like she had met everyone important and done everything the world had to offer. Now was not one of those times.

"We ask the makers of this world to listen," Libra said. The Pyxians fell silent and bent their heads.

"The makers . . . " Suzanne whispered. To Brit the meaning was clear enough. Libra was talking about Suzanne. The Pyxians thought their world was designed. It wasn't that different from most religions in the real world, except that Brit knew the Pyxians were right. She remembered how uncomfortable she had felt first hearing this from Burgrave.

"We will not ask them for victory. But we want them to watch as we seize victory for ourselves!"

Libra stood on a raised platform, flanked by her brother and sister. The queen wore the same flowing robe as always, her crown little more than a metal circlet resting on her forehead. With her last words, she spread her arms wide and the crowd roared their approval.

Lynx and Leo also wore the undecorated robes, but Brit noticed right away that they were both armed. Leo clutched his stave as his eyes scanned the crowd. When the rest of the Pyxians closed their eyes, swaying with the energy of the moment, the prince remained hawkeyed as ever. Lynx was also on guard, but she managed it with a smile as opposed to her brother's scowl.

That guy needs to lighten up, Brit thought. *Ramses wouldn't be dumb enough to try anything here.*

Ramses had no reason to try anything, regardless. After Libra sent back her terms with the envoy, Dante, Ramses's response had come quickly. He refused Libra's terms. As was Ramses's right, his refusal came with the specifications for the trial by combat. Each kingdom would field seven representatives to fight one on one in a best-of-seven match. To Brit, the whole thing sounded like it was a mix between a WWE grudge match and one of Perry Hall High's sports meets.

Then does that make this the pep rally? she wondered. Brit had ditched every pep rally since starting high school. They always seemed like bullshit to her. Why get all hyped up for some football game or wrestling match? Yet the atmosphere of this Pyxian ceremony was infectious, and Brit found herself unconsciously chanting along with the NPCs once or twice. *Maybe it's because I never gave a shit about our football team*, Brit mused.

The Duels, as the NPCs around camp had started calling the trial by combat, were to take place in a week. Libra still hadn't announced who the seven representatives were for Pyxis, although Brit assumed that the queen and her siblings were going to fight. That left four spots, one of which Brit was determined to get. She wasn't going to sit and watch as someone else fought with her life on the line.

Ramses had set the time, so Libra got to choose

the place. At the start of the ceremony, the queen announced the fights were to take place at some lake deep in the south of Io called The Floating Eye. Suze only shrugged when she heard the name, but that didn't really surprise Brit. The amount Suzanne knew about Io seemed to shrink every day. *It doesn't matter where we fight*, Brit told herself, *all that matters is that we win.*

The ceremony was winding down. NPCs headed back: some to their tents, the sentries to their posts. Many stayed in the center of the camp, talking or standing silent, still caught in the magic of the ceremony. Libra left the podium, followed by her siblings, and the crowd began to disperse.

Brit hopped off the cart and stretched.

"Where are you going?" Mikayla asked.

"To sign up," Brit answered. Ever since that afternoon in the woods, they had avoided talking about The Duels with each other. Still, Brit was glad when her friends slid down from the cart and jogged to keep up with her.

Pyxians stepped aside as the three of them cut through the crowd toward Libra. A few, most Citizens, waved hello or offered words of encouragement to the girls. Brit figured they were Altairis she had helped cross the river. Were there really so many of them? She didn't remember helping that many NPCs, but the weeks of visiting Altair must have added up.

They caught up to Libra just as the queen broke free of the crowd. "Wait up!" Brit shouted. Leo whipped around, his stave ready, but he relaxed as soon as he saw Suzanne.

They stepped away from the crowd toward Libra's tent, exchanging pleasantries about the ceremony.

"I am glad you chose to attend," the queen said.

"It was incredible," Mikayla answered earnestly.

"Listen," Brit cut in. If she didn't stop Mikayla now, they'd spend all night complimenting the queen and Brit would never get to what really mattered. "I've got to be one of the seven. For The Duels."

"Got to?" Libra raised an eyebrow.

Brit didn't flinch. "Yeah. Remember back in Vale when we signed on with you guys? You promised you would help us if you could, and now you can. Let me fight. That's all the help I need."

Brit thought she saw Libra's mouth twitch up into a smile, but just as quickly the queen had turned toward Suzanne and was asking her if she also wanted to be one of the seven. Suzanne glanced at Brit before answering.

"Yes," she said. "There's no way I'm missing the look on Ramses face when he sees us beat his champions down."

Everyone turned toward Mikayla. She hesitated. Brit knew Mikayla hated all the fighting, and she wondered if this time Mikayla was really going to sit things out. But Mikayla simply said, "I want to fight, too." She didn't give a reason, but Brit knew she didn't have to. Either Libra was going to choose them or she wasn't.

"I was waiting for the three of you to ask," Libra said. "I feel much relieved knowing Pyxis will have champions such as you."

Brit let out a loud whoop of excitement and Suzanne gave a little fist pump. Only Mikayla remembered her courtesy and thanked the queen. The queen smiled and excused herself, leaving behind her siblings. Brit was about to make fun of Mikayla for being a perfect Ms. Manners, even now, when she noticed something odd.

Her experience points were increasing.

And not just a little bit. Three days ago Brit had hit the threshold for level nineteen. She'd gone through her menu to see which of her stats had increased and to see how far it was to level twenty. The threshold for the next level was so high it staggered her. She'd made a little progress, but she thought she would have to grind for the rest of the week if she wanted to level up before The Duels took place.

That was clearly not the case anymore. She couldn't see Suze or Mikayla's experience, but from the way they were staring a little to the left, she could guess they were watching their own points rocket upward. The little number at the bottom left of Brit's vision grew larger and larger until it hit the threshold for level twenty.

After all those previous level ups, Brit knew what to expect, but this time everything felt way more intense. The sensation began at her belly button and spread outward until it felt like her whole body was vibrating with energy. Her muscles flexed and relaxed and flexed again, and she felt hot, almost feverish. Brit closed her eyes and told herself it would all be over soon. Right when it became almost too much to bear, the sensation stopped.

Brit tried to open her eyes, but she couldn't. She tried to shout to Mikayla for help but her character's mouth couldn't form the words. It was like when a controller malfunctioned on an old gaming console—no matter what she tried to do, nothing was responding.

Then her shoulders grew heavier, like someone had stacked weights on them. The weight spread to her arms and down her torso to her hips. She felt her entire body inflating and thicker muscles sprouting on top of her old ones. Finally, when she had felt even her feet grow, she regained control of her body.

Brit wasn't ready and promptly collapsed in a heap. She heard Suze and Mikayla collapsing next to her, but she couldn't help them before she figured out what was happening to her.

Blinking, Brit managed to push herself onto her hands and knees. She found her feet and rose unsteadily. Once she was standing, she looked down, and almost lost her balance again. Had the ground always been that far away? And when did Lynx and Leo get so short?

She saw Mikayla gawking at her. Brit gawked right back. Mikayla was definitely taller. Her arms were longer, too: hanging at her side they stretched down to her knees. Even her clothing looked different. She'd been wearing leggings and a padded cotton shirt, but now she wore something that looked halfway between a karate gi and a pantsuit.

And Suzanne had also changed, her Rogue's cloak replaced with a longer one that draped over her shoulders. Brit couldn't see where any part of Suzanne was beneath the cloak. If she didn't stare right at Suzanne, Suze seemed to disappear into the shadows of the tents.

"Are you okay?" Lynx asked, eying them warily. Leo took a step toward Suzanne to steady her. "What made you all fall?"

"You mean you can't see?" Brit asked. She was going to say more but Mikayla shook her head in warning. Brit caught her drift. If the twins had noticed the changes, they would have made some comment about them.

"We're fine," Mikayla said. It was a weak lie and neither of the Pyxians seemed to buy it. Still, neither of them challenged the girls when Suzanne said they had to go talk amongst themselves. Brit stumbled a few times as they walked back to their tent, unused to the length of her legs and her new center of gravity.

She had to duck to get into the tent. She'd had to duck before, but now she was basically bowing as she followed Suzanne and Mikayla inside.

"What the fuck?" she shouted, stopping when she remembered the NPCs could hear through the tents and dropped her voice to a whisper. "What the fuck just happened?"

Suzanne looked like a mad scientist. "We changed classes! Check your stats, it should tell you what you are now."

Brit had been expecting the class change, but she thought her stats would change, not her entire body. She looked at her new massive hands and flexed the fingers. She could do some serious damage with these.

She flipped open her menu and checked out her stats. Underneath her name, where it had previously said Fighter, it now said Dragoon. Checking her skills she saw she could now wield two-handed weapons with one hand, and that her unarmed strikes were almost twice as powerful as before.

She reported the changes to the others as they puzzled over the differences in their own characters. "I'm a Swiftblade," Mikayla said, looking more confused than anything else. "Apparently, I don't fight with shields anymore and I'm supposed to get another sword."

Suze was a kid in a candy store. "This is so fucking cool," she laughed. "I'm an Infiltrator! I wanted to see how these would play!"

"I wonder why Lynx and Leo didn't notice the changes," Mikayla said.

"Why would they?" Suzanne replied. "They recognize us, not our characters. I don't think they even know what we look like really, just who we are."

"Well, that explains why Leo would be down to date you in the first place," Brit quipped. Mikayla rolled her eyes.

"Very funny," Suzanne said, launching into a lengthy explanation of all the skills and abilities of their new classes. Brit managed to pay attention while Suze described the Dragoon's abilities, but when Suzanne went into how Swiftblades could use a hit-combo to reset their cool-down, Brit started zoning out. *It's nice to know that some things never change*, she thought.

Chapter 10

The Ion River rushed to the east, its tumbling waters near black in the fading dusk light. Brit led the way south. Even in the low light, Suzanne could easily make out Brit's shape. They would have to stop soon or else it would get so dark that even Mikayla wouldn't be able to see.

Suzanne sped up to catch up with Mikayla. She tapped her on the shoulder and Mikayla jumped, startled.

"Sorry!" Suzanne said. "When do you think we should stop?"

Mikayla ignored her question. "How did you sneak up on me like that? I didn't hear you at all."

"I'll try to be noisier next time," Suzanne replied. Now that she was an Infiltrator, her footsteps didn't make any sound, and the long black cloak that came with her class helped her blend into shadows even better.

"Seriously," Mikayla continued, "you almost gave me a heart attack. There's a clearing in the trees up ahead. We should stop there for the night. We'll have the river to the east, and we'll hear anybody trying to come through the trees. Unless they're Infiltrators, I guess."

They set up a quick camp. Brit volunteered to take the first watch. Suzanne pulled a tent out of her inventory and set it up, thinking about how weird it was to be sleeping out in the wilderness again. They'd spent so long at the Pyxian camp, constantly surrounded by NPCs, that she'd almost forgotten what it was like roughing it in Io. She never thought she would miss her stiff cot, but uncomfortable as it was, it still beat sleeping on the ground.

When she changed into an Infiltrator, she gained about an inch, enough so that her feet had hung off the edge of the cot. That was easy enough to solve by curling up her knees, but Brit's problem wasn't that easily fixed. Already her cot was bigger than the other girls, and once she became a Dragoon, even that wasn't enough. Brit's arms and legs hung over the edges and if she rolled onto her side, the cot was likely to flip under her bulk.

Suzanne shifted her weight, trying to find a more comfortable position on her pad. She would be lying if she told herself she wasn't excited by the prospect of traveling through Io again. Mikayla had suggested they only ride part of the way downriver with Libra and her entourage. It would give them more time to get used to their new classes, Mikayla had argued, but Suzanne suspected her friend was just trying to put off getting to The Floating Eye. Mikayla was right, though. Suzanne had stumbled a few times just walking today, and they hadn't even fought yet in their new bodies. It would all take some getting used to, and it was good that they would have this time before they fought in The Duels.

Suzanne closed her eyes. She woke up to Mikayla shaking her shoulder, rousing her for her watch. Dawn was yet to break, but the sky was lightening. Suzanne stretched, her back a little sore from the stiff ground, and stood up to take her spot by the edge of the forest.

After a few uneventful hours, Brit and Mikayla got up. They broke camp and resumed the trek south. They had walked for most of the morning when Brit suddenly burst out laughing. They had to stop and wait for her to calm down. Her body trembled from laughing and after she stopped she was so out of breath she had to lean against a tree while she caught her breath.

"You okay?" Suzanne asked, eying her warily.

Brit nodded, panting. "It's just . . . remember pop quizzes?"

And then she laughed again, almost as hard

as before. Mikayla started laughing too and soon Suzanne found herself joining them. Brit put her back to the tree and slid to a seat on the ground.

"Remember hall passes?" she asked. "Like we couldn't even go to the bathroom without someone telling us it was okay."

"What made you think about hall passes?" Suzanne asked, chuckling.

Brit shrugged. "That Pyxian sing-along right before we left. I don't know, it just kind of seemed like a pep rally, you know? Like they were all getting hyped up for a football game."

"It's pretty much the same thing," Mikayla said. She stuck out a hand for Brit and Suzanne did the same. Pulling together, the two of them lifted her back up to standing. They set off again, although this time at more of a stroll than before, trading memories from the real world.

"I never went to a game," Suzanne confessed. "Not homecoming or when we made the state championships or anything."

"Good," Brit said. "That's something to be proud of."

"I just always thought that was for the cool kids, you know? Like if I showed up, they'd make me sit with the other team's fans."

"You weren't missing anything," Mikayla said bitterly. "Trust me. I went to so many fucking games. Football, basketball. We had to go to track meets sometimes. You know how boring a track meet is?"

"I forgot all the horrors of the cheer squad," Suzanne said.

"You don't know the half of it."

"Neither do you," Brit laughed. "You spent all those games staring at the fans, right? So how many did you actually watch?"

That got a chuckle out of Mikayla. "Enough. More than enough. It sucks watching a team lose and lose while you're trying to amp everyone up. The fans knew the cheers are bullshit because we sucked so bad. Like damn, put me in. I would've been better than most of those kids."

"Well, at least you looked good watching them lose," Brit joked. Mikayla rolled her eyes, but Suzanne thought she saw the ghost of a smile playing on Mikayla's lips as she turned back toward the woods.

"Something's coming out of the woods," Mikayla said.

"NPCs?" Suzanne asked, pulling out her daggers. She couldn't see anything yet.

"Monsters." Mikayla's swords were in her hands. She still wasn't very good with her left hand yet, but there was nothing like a little hands-on experience to get better.

"Good," Brit said. "Time for you to get in the game."

Suzanne could hear the monsters now. A loud humming sound came out of the forest, droning over the sound of whatever it was moving through the trees. Then she saw them: huge insects, wings beating so fast they were a blur. They were like beetles, armored in a shiny black carapace, with an equally tough bit of exoskeleton covering their heads. In place of their front legs were two scythe-like claws that hacked branches out of the way as they flew for the girls.

"What the fuck are these things?" Brit shouted, readying her halberd.

"Swordbeetles!" Suzanne shouted back. Before she could say anything else the beetles were upon them.

One dive-bombed for Suzanne and she rolled out of the way. The beetle's claws left two deep gouges in the earth where she had stood. She threw herself on the beetle's back and stabbed down with a dagger, but the blade glanced off the hard carapace without leaving so much as a scratch. The monster bucked and Suzanne held tight with her legs. It couldn't take off with her weight on its back, but nothing prevented it from trying to slam her into a tree. She flipped over its head right before it could pin her between its carapace and a trunk, stabbing at its underbelly. It screeched as her blade sunk in, but then it slashed at her with its claws and she had to throw herself out of the way, leaving the dagger embedded in its abdomen.

She looked to her left and saw Mikayla engaged in a swordfight with another beetle, her twin blades parrying its twin claws. Another beetle joined the fight and now Mikayla was fighting four blades with two.

The stabbed beetle took to the air again, charging Suzanne. She heard Brit shout, "Duck!" and hit the ground. The monster zoomed over her head and Brit swung her halberd like a flyswatter, smacking it down. Even through its armor, the attack did significant damage. Suzanne dashed over to the stunned monster and finished it off with another quick stab to its underbelly.

Once it was reduced to pixels, her embedded dagger dropped free. Just in time: another beetle was swinging a claw at her and Suzanne barely got her daggers up in time to block. She heard another screech coming from Mikayla's direction and knew that one of her blades had found its way through a beetle's guard. The monster in front of Suzanne didn't give her time to look. It lowered its head and tried to bowl her over. Suzanne placed her hands on its head and vaulted the monster, giving a kick as she flew over. The beetle's momentum led it to crash into a tree. Brit finished off the dazed monster before it could recover.

That left only the one Mikayla was fighting. Thrust and parry, hack and slash, Suzanne watched her friend drive the monster backwards. The beetle slashed at Mikayla with its right claw, but instead of catching the claw on her sword Mikayla stepped to the side. The beetle's claw dug into the ground and stuck there. When the monster tried to slash at her with its left claw, Mikayla caught it between her two blades. Then she closed them like scissors and chopped the monster's claw right off. Whirling around, she slashed across its thorax with one blade and the abdomen with another. A quick stab to the head and the beetle joined the other monsters in becoming pixels.

And just like that, there was quiet. No wings beat against the air, no beetles screeched and there were no sounds of steel meeting claw, blade meeting carapace. Aside from the river, everything was still.

Suzanne stuck her daggers back in her inventory and walked over to grab some loot. The beetles dropped the material that formed their carapaces when they died, and Suzanne figured she could try forging it into something when they got back to the Pyxian camp.

"You want any of this?" she asked Brit.

"Nah," Brit said, still clutching her halberd. "You good, Mikayla?"

Mikayla didn't respond. She was listening intently, her head cocked toward the forest. "Something else is in there," she muttered. She stalked toward the trees, her hand on the hilt of her sword.

Another beetle came screaming out of the woods. Before it got close to Mikayla, Suzanne saw something collide with its side. The force of impact threw it on its side, and Mikayla was on it before it could cover its underbelly. While she dispatched the monster, Suzanne turned to face whoever had knocked it out of the air.

A tall NPC stepped out of the forest. He had a one-handed axe strapped to his waist, just like the one he had thrown at the beetle. He wore a sleeveless shirt that showed off the muscles on his arms and wide-legged pants.

"I was wondering if I might run into you three," he said, a smile breaking out on his face.

"Alphonse!" Suzanne was stoked to see the NPC again. The last time she had seen Alphonse was at the start of the war. When the Pyxian armies left Vale, Alphonse had stayed behind as regent. He was fiercely loyal, and a fierce fighter with his axes, as the beetles could attest.

Brit clapped Alphonse on the back. "Great to

see you, Al. How'd you know where we would be?"

"I did not. Libra sent word as soon as Ramses contacted her about the peace. She feared it might come down to ritual combat and requested I head toward The Floating Eye."

"You mean you're fighting in The Duels?" Mikayla asked.

Alphonse smiled a grim grin. "It is my honor to fight once more for Pyxis. There is much I owe Ramses that I would repay."

Is he talking about Collette? Suzanne wondered.

Collette was another Pyxian who had fought alongside the girls and Alphonse in Vale. There seemed to be something between Alphonse and Collette, but the battle in Vale had taken Collette's life. None of the girls had been particularly fond of Collette, and Collette had never trusted Suzanne or her friends. But that didn't mean Suzanne celebrated the NPC's death.

With Alphonse in tow they set off again, heading

south along the river. After walking in silence for a minute, Alphonse said, "While I traveled here, I passed by Pyxia. The banner of Ramses still hangs over our Capital."

"Libra said she'd rebuild Pyxia when the war was over," Mikayla said. "But first she wants to free land."

"The land will not be free as long as one foul pixel of Ramses's presence remains," Alphonse replied. "Every day those banners hang dishonors our fallen . . . " There was a distant look in his eye as his voice trailed off. Suzanne knew he must be thinking about Collette.

"Well, it's a good thing we're heading to The Floating Eye," Brit said. "We'll kick Ramses's ass so bad he won't be able to sit on that fancy throne of his anymore. And then we're going to tear down all those banners and shove them down his throat."

Alphonse laughed. "I find myself, not for the first time, quite happy you are on our side of this war."

Chapter 11

"No way," Mikayla said, taking a step back. "No freaking way."

For once, Brit didn't think Mikayla was being chicken. "You're nuts," she said to Alphonse. "If we jump we're going to die."

They stood at the end of the Ion River. After traveling it for so long, first in a boat, and then by foot, Brit wasn't sure the river had an end. But soon into their march that morning they heard a great roaring to the south. Around noon, the horizon dropped away into nothing. They were approaching the limit of Io's continent. Brit could tell it was making Suzanne giddy with implications. *At least Alphonse is here,* Brit thought. With an NPC around, Suzanne had to keep her designer talk to a minimum.

Then they had seen the river's end. All the way from the north of the map, water rushed down the Ion River. Once the river reached its terminus, the water had nowhere to go but down.

Down it went, huge cascades of water falling into a thick grey mist. Staring over the edge into the grey made Brit's stomach lurch. She could only imagine how far it fell. Skydiving had always intrigued her, but it wasn't like they had parachutes or anything.

The falls made so much noise they needed to shout to be heard. "We can't even see where it goes," Mikayla shouted. "And you want us to jump?"

Alphonse nodded. All the way there, he had said that the way to The Floating Eye was to follow the river. That included following the river off a cliff, apparently.

Brit would have liked for there to be another way down. She shot Suzanne a quizzical look, but Suzanne was peering into the mist, trying to discern what sort of landing waited for them. She asked Mikayla, "Can you see anything?"

Mikayla shook her head. "Just more mist."

Great, Brit thought. *We're totally blind.*

"What will we do when we hit the bottom?" Suzanne asked. "It's not like we can swim or anything."

"It requires a leap of faith," Alphonse answered. "I can go first, if you'd like."

It figured. They had just gotten used to their new classes and the new bodies that came with them. Every time they thought they'd got the hang of things, something threw a wrench in their plans. Brit trusted Alphonse. They'd fought side by side against the Altairi Army, but maybe the Pyxian had snapped. Maybe he was going to throw himself to his death and wanted to take the girls with him. Maybe he figured the war was a lost cause and this was the easiest way to end it. Or maybe a magical pegasus would fly down and snag them out of the air before they fell to oblivion.

The *maybes* hung in the air as thick as the fog. There has to be another way down, Brit told herself. Suzanne wouldn't design something like this. But one look at Suzanne's face told her that Suzanne had designed none of this—The Floating Eye, the waterfall, and shit, even the war was some fluke in programming. They could argue about it for days, but in the end, either they were going to jump, or they weren't.

"I'll go first then," Alphonse said. He walked to the edge of the waterfall and stepped forward into the nothingness. His body pierced a hole in the mist that was quickly covered up by the swirling grey.

None of the girls spoke. Then Mikayla burst out laughing.

"We're going to follow him, aren't we?"

Brit found herself grinning. She grabbed Suzanne and Mikayla by the arms and half-led, half-dragged her friends over the edge.

They fell. Brit held tight on their arms. She could feel Mikayla shaking, the wind pulling against their bodies as it resisted their descent, but all she could see was the grey mist whipping past, and all she could hear was the roar of the falls. Something inside her told her not to let go. She counted to a hundred while they fell, and they kept falling, so she kept counting. She had counted to a thousand, blind and deafened, drenched by spray, when she realized that they were slowing down.

But that would be absurd. Their deceleration had to be some trick of limbo. Brit figured she'd lost perspective, that was all. But then she felt Mikayla tugging at her arm, mouthing some words that were lost to the wind and waterfall. *Is she feeling it too?* Brit wondered. Mikayla gestured frantically with her free hand, but the mist had grown so thick that Brit couldn't make out her fingers.

Yet there was no denying it. They had to be slowing down. And then the fog began to thin below her and Brit saw The Floating Eye.

It was like looking out the window of an

airplane, except the window was below her and she was falling toward the ground. Well, not ground, but water. They fell toward a massive lake, filled by the falling waters of the Ion River. In the middle, like the pupil of an eye, was a perfectly round island. Surrounding the clear lake waters was a stony shore.

That'd be a bitch to hit, Brit thought. Luckily, they were falling for the lake water. Still, hadn't she heard that falling into water from this height was like hitting concrete? Even if she managed to live, she didn't think she'd be in any shape to fight after breaking every bone in her body.

But, of course, she wouldn't break every bone in her body. Here in Io, she didn't think her body even had any bones. The realization made her giddy, or maybe that was the adrenaline from falling, or maybe she was nuts after all, crazy to jump off a waterfall, and these were going to be her last thoughts before they hit. Even though they were slowing down, Brit knew they were still going way too fast to survive the impact. Their characters took falling damage, after all, and none of them had ever fallen a tenth of this distance.

They were a hundred feet above the lake, then fifty. Then, at twenty feet, Brit felt something catch her—an invisible force that stopped their descent. For a second, they hung suspended in the air, fifteen feet above the water. That was when the surprise made Brit let go of her friends. Then whatever magical game engine held them up let them go, and they dropped the last distance, landing in the lake with a huge splash.

The water felt like it was wet and also like it was dry. Brit mouth's fell open and she swallowed but nothing ran down her throat. It was like floating in thicker air, like nothing at all. She kicked toward the surface and her knees hit the sandy bottom of the lake. This close to shore the water was only a foot deep.

"Where are you guys?" Suzanne asked. Brit looked around for her voice but couldn't find her through the thick mist. She floundered in the shadows, crawling back to shore. There was Suzanne. She was completely dry, as if she hadn't just jumped off a waterfall into a lake. Brit looked down and realized her gear was dry as well. *This just gets weirder and weirder*, she thought.

"You see Mikayla?" she asked Suzanne.

Suzanne shook her head. "I can't see anything."

Brit thought she saw shapes coming toward shore but they turned out to be tricks of the mist. Where was Mikayla? She was about to get really worried when Mikayla came strolling up onto the bank like nothing had happened.

"Where were you?" Brit asked.

"In the lake," Mikayla replied, like it was the most obvious thing in the world. Which, upon reflection, it clearly was.

"Where are you all?" Alphonse's voice boomed over the lake.

"On the shore!" Mikayla yelled back. Brit motioned for her to take the lead. Even if they couldn't see, Brit knew that Mikayla could follow Alphonse's voice way better than anyone else.

Stumbling over the shore, they made their way around the lake to Alphonse. Once they had walked a quarter of the way around the lake they found him waiting at a narrow stone bridge, stretching from the shore to the island in the center. Brit couldn't make out the vague shapes on the island.

They walked single file across the bridge. The stone was slick with water and the footing uneven. More than once Brit felt herself wobble and had to stop until she regained her balance. At one point she heard Suzanne shout, "Shit!" and then a loud splash. She felt the water splash onto her back and turned to see Suze pulling herself back onto the bridge. She caught Mikayla's eye and almost broke into a grin, but then Brit stumbled and figured she should make sure she got across before they did anything else.

She focused on putting one foot in front of the other, and before she knew it, they had reached the island. Brit stepped off the bridge onto firmer ground. Finally, she could get a better look at where The Duels were taking place.

The pupil of The Floating Eye lay flat. Lake water lapped at the edges, some spilling over onto the pupil. As they walked toward the center, Brit saw that the island was almost entirely barren. There were no trees or any other kind of vegetation. The island was made of white marble. More than once Brit slipped on the water-slicked stone. *This is going to be tricky for fighting*, she thought.

The only structures appeared to be NPC made. It was like the Pyxian camp in miniature: tents set up in a ring around a forge. Everything beyond the Pyxian camp was shrouded in more of the mist. Brit wondered if it would ever dissipate.

But between the girls and the Pyxian camp were dueling grounds. The grounds were a depressed circle hewn from the island's marble. The circle was painted blue. At the center of this circle was a smaller circle, chalk white, bisected by a thick black line. Alphonse explained that each fight started with both combatants standing on either side of that line.

Stadium seating, stone steps, and benches, flanked the circle on the north and south sides. Brit wondered if anyone was coming to fill the crowds. She didn't think any of the Pyxians had come besides the champions, and the thought of fighting in front of a crowd of hostile Altairi was slightly nauseating.

"Suzanne!" Leo shouted, his voice cutting through the fog. Suzanne sped up, much to Brit's amusement, jogging toward the prince. Brit caught Mikayla's eye and smirked. Mikayla shook her head. Brit never knew what to expect in Io—add Suzanne running after an NPC to that list.

By the time they reached the tents, the rest of the Pyxians had appeared. Besides the public display of affection that was Leo and Suze's reunion, Lynx and Libra greeted them warmly. The queen and Alphonse went off to talk about the state of

Vale, leaving Brit and Mikayla with her siblings and the other members of their entourage.

Rigel and Hollis had also come along to run the forge for any last-minute repairs and tune-ups. Brit recognized a couple of older NPCs from the Pyxian camp, healers she'd never really interacted with before. She mumbled hellos but didn't have much more to say than she did back in Pyxis.

So Brit went to explore the last bit of the pupil. Tied up on the shore was the boat the Pyxians arrived in. Brit wondered if they had ridden the boat over the edge of the waterfall to get down here. Mikayla found her there, staring off the boat at the distant shore.

"This place is nuts."

"Just this place?" Mikayla laughed softly. "All of Io is nuts. Didn't you realize?"

"Yeah, but this is even nuttier. This is trail mix."

"This is nut brittle," Mikayla said.

They stood for a second in silence. The mist faded away, revealing the rest of the lake around them. The far side of the lake, opposite the water-fall, remained shrouded in fog. Brit supposed that was the actual end of the world and wondered what would happen if she went over there.

She couldn't think about that. They were here to fight, here to win. But not yet. Brit sat down with her feet in the wet-and-dry water. Mikayla joined her. They sat in silence, together, at the edge of the virtual world.

A huge splash broke the calm. Brit jumped to attention and saw a huge ship glide down out of the sky, drifting down from the waterfall. This wasn't a little dinghy like Lynx and Leo's boat, but a proper sailing ship with multiple masts and a web of rigging hooked up to its sails. Four pillars were stamped on each sail, a crimson orb on top of each. The boat landed in The Floating Eye with a splash that sent waves all the way to the pupil. Brit knew that it had to be Ramses and his champions arriving from Altair.

Chapter 12

Suzanne watched the ship fall. Its sails fluttered in the wind as it glided down into the water. The physics engine at The Floating Eye was completely wonky; anywhere else in Io the ship would have dropped like a stone, breaking apart after taking so much falling damage. *Maybe not anywhere else,* Suzanne reminded herself. *You didn't know about this place and you don't know what else is out there.*

Well, she knew one thing for certain. The Altairi ship cutting through the lake water carried Ramses and his retinue, the seven champions of Altair. They would be at The Eye's pupil soon.

Suzanne walked back toward the dueling grounds to join up with the other champions of Pyxis.

She found Leo sitting with his twin by the center of the circles. Leo spoke to Lynx in hushed tones, breaking off the conversation when he saw Suzanne approach. "I was wondering where you went," he said. To Suzanne, he sounded a little too cheerful, a little forced. Lynx acknowledged her with a slight smile.

She wanted to ask, "What were you talking about?" But they were obviously whispering for a reason, and the last thing Suzanne wanted was to start some kind of argument. Leave the fighting for The Duels. Now was the time for waiting nervously.

Libra and Alphonse joined them. Libra looked a little queasy. Suzanne had seen the queen angry before, and elated, but this was the first time Libra had ever appeared to be nervous. While the other NPCs filled the time with nervous chatter, Libra remained silent, pacing slowly around the perimeter of the innermost white ring.

Suzanne thought the pupil of The Floating Eye was beautiful, especially the dueling grounds. The circles were perfectly round, the colored sections without any kind of texture or blemish. This was not something she had designed, she knew, at least not on purpose. It could have been some unfinished file she'd stuck under the map, too lazy to properly store it away. As to how the NPCs had found The Floating Eye, Suzanne could only guess.

The huge sails loomed ever closer. Brit and Mikayla showed up, wordlessly slipping in with the rest of the Pyxian champions. Suzanne stared at the massive ship, wondering how many NPCs Ramses had brought with him. What if this was just an ambush that they had stupidly run into? She couldn't believe she had trusted Ramses to keep his word after all the crap he'd pulled already.

And then the Altairi arrived.

The Altairi ship beached on the opposite side

of the pupil from the Pyxian tents. A gangplank slid down from the deck of the ship and a procession of Zenith Citizens, wrapped in their foppery, filed out onto the shore. They formed two rows on either side of the gangplank. Then, as if on cue, they began to loudly applaud. Ramses, king of Altair, strutted down onto the marble. He walked to the dueling grounds, stopping at the edge of the blue circle.

He wore his blood-red robes and crimson crown. His gray face was curled up in a mocking smile and his hand rested on the jeweled hilt of a gilded sword, the kind of useless plaything merchants sold in Zenith City. He surveyed the assembled Pyxians with a look of utter contempt.

"Greetings, Libra," he said in his odd, high voice. "I had hoped you drowned on the way here, but I see I suffer no such luck."

"Ramses," she replied. Her voice betrayed no emotion, but Suzanne could see the fury in the queen's eyes.

Ramses's lip curled, halfway between a snarl and a sneer. His pale eyes surveyed the Pyxians, coming to rest on Suzanne, Brit, and Mikayla. "I see Pyxis suffers for lack of defenders! Is your kingdom in such a sorry state that you needed murderers and liars to defend you?"

"Have you come to insult us, Ramses, or have you come to decide this conflict?" Leo asked, stepping forward.

"Who is to say I cannot do both? Heathens, I have the pleasure of introducing to you the seven great heroes of Altair."

Suzanne wasn't surprised to see Burgrave walking down the gangplank. The short, bald NPC wore the flowing grey robe of the Pyxians, which made sense, as he was Pyxian-born. His two earrings, rubies on long silver chains, swung in the breeze as he crossed to stand beside his king. Burgrave was a skilled fighter, Suzanne knew, though only by reputation. She had watched him disarm Brit once, and that had happened faster than she could blink. She wasn't looking forward to fighting against him now.

The next NPC Suzanne recognized as the captain of the Zenith City Guard. Ramses introduced him as Crux. He was huge, dwarfing Brit in size. He carried a gigantic maul slung over his shoulder. The entire ship rocked whenever the Altairi Dragoon took a step. Yet despite his fearsome size, he had a soft face. He bounded down the gangplank and formed up beside Burgrave.

None of the next three were known to Suzanne. First came an Assassin draped in a long black cloak, their features completely obscured by a mask. The mask was painted white and was expressionless except for two eyeholes and a slit by the mouth. Ramses introduced the Assassin as Gemini.

He called his next champion Hydrus. He looked like a common Sellsword to Suzanne, but that couldn't be right. Why would Ramses bring a Sellsword to fight against the best that Pyxis had to offer? Even before they reached their advanced classes, Suzanne and her friends could have crushed any Sellsword. Now that they had changed class this Hydrus didn't stand a chance.

Hydrus bowed to the Pyxians. His eyes looked almost lidless and his nose was flat and narrow, little more than two flared nostrils on his face. He smiled a wide, tight-lipped smile, which made Suzanne all the more uncomfortable.

Ramses introduced the fifth champion as Xenos. Suzanne couldn't guess the NPC's class, or anything else about him. A hood cast the Altairi's face in shadow. He held his hands together, long sleeves joining in the front to hide his hands. *Under that hooded cloak he could be anything*, Suzanne thought.

After Xenos, no others came. "Where are they?" Ramses demanded.

It was Xenos who answered in a dispassionate voice. "They will come soon, my liege. They were held up arming themselves."

Who they were became clear enough when Suzanne saw a familiar face lumbering down the gangplank. The sixth champion was a massive defender, though nowhere near as large as the Dragoon Crux. The Defender walked side by side with the seventh champion, a slender Sniper carrying a bow taller than herself.

Suzanne heard Mikayla begin to ask, "Isn't that . . . " Her voice trailed off.

Brit finished the sentence for her. "Samara and Desmond."

Suzanne hadn't seen either of the Altairi since they had all killed the Lamia together, back when the girls still quested for Ramses. Samara, Desmond, and the third member of their party, a Troubadour named Picciotto, had disappeared as soon as the Mongrels attacked the girls. That felt like a lifetime ago. Suzanne wondered what had happened to the mercenaries, and at her trial was told that the three of them had fled. So what were they doing here now? And where was Picciotto?

And why were Samara and Desmond regarding her and her friends like they had never seen them before, sizing them up like they were any other enemy? They weren't enemies, they were allies, weren't they? Suzanne remembered Samara ripping on Ramses back when they were all in the king's employ. It was hardly believable that they would fight for him now.

Samara and Desmond had also been way livelier than the blank-faced NPCs who stood in front of Suzanne now. Even Desmond, who was a Defender of few words, found ways to make his silence sarcastic. But now he waited like a huge lapdog for orders from a king Suzanne knew he despised.

She was so consumed by her thoughts that she didn't look up when Libra said her name as one of Pyxis' champions. A few more pithy remarks from Ramses and the Altairi turned and walked back to their ships, followed by the procession of Zenith Citizens.

Chapter 13

Suzanne breathed in the mist of morning. Swirling off the surface of the lake, creeping around the dueling grounds, cloaking the horizon—in the early hours, mist ruled The Floating Eye, blanketing all she could see in grey. Shadows moved through the mist, but she could not tell if they were just phantoms of the fog or something more corporeal. She supposed it didn't matter, not really. All that mattered were the fights to be fought, the seven duels that would decide the fates of Pyxis and Altair and her own fate as well.

It's funny, she thought. *How small it all seems.*

In Zenith City there were thousands of NPCs, thousands more scattered across Pyxis, yet all that mattered to Suzanne were the fourteen champions who would be fighting in The Duels. *And Ramses*, she reminded herself. This was all happening because of the machinations of the king. Whom she had created.

Lately, she was having to remind herself of that more and more. There was just so much to this world she had never planned for, so much that constantly surprised her. Like The Floating Eye. She still didn't understand where it came from, but she knew it had to be a result of the code she'd written, because everything in Io was. Well, either a result of her code or a result of how her code interacted with the TII.

Reflexively her hands went up to her head and felt for the TII that was and was not there. In the real world, she was wearing a TII and the device was what made the entire world appear before her. But she couldn't feel the TII in Io. She could only feel what it told her to feel. Right now it told her she was chilly from the cold air blowing off The Floating Eye. It told her the air was filled with mist and she felt the damp creeping up her nose and into her stomach.

She knew she was really in her room, breathing stale air, trapped in some kind of dreamlike trance. But *really* is a tricky word: she could feel and hear the world of Io around her, while her bedroom was something like a memory of a half-forgotten dream. And she could hear the footsteps of Leo approaching, she could see him emerging from the mists. She could feel the hand he put on her shoulder, his lips kissing her softly on the cheek. She could hear him say, "It's time to get ready," see the gentle way he looked at her. She could feel the unyielding stone of the island beneath her as she walked, the apprehension in her chest.

She knew that she was about to fight for her friends and her freedom. A million concerns about the battle consumed her—what weapons to bring, who she'd be fighting, how she'd be fighting. Distracted, her mind forgot that this wasn't real, this was all an illusion of the TII. She forgot that she was not *really* an Infiltrator, a wanted criminal, a champion of Pyxis.

She was all of those things. And she was nervous, a little afraid, but beyond that excited and tired of waiting. The night before she had gone to sleep instantly, as always happened in Io. However, even if the sleep came quickly, she never had dreams to hold her there. So she had risen and left her tent with the sun still working its way through the mists of morning, and now she was returning to her tent to finish preparing.

She reached into her inventory and withdrew her armor—thick leather, reinforced with small plates of metal. She put reinforced greaves over her leggings. They took away some of her stealth, but in The Duels there would be nowhere to hide. Her boots had steel toes to make her kicks strong and soft soles to make her steps silent.

She equipped a sturdy belt around her waist and sheathed her two curved daggers. Two smaller belts crossed over her chest, studded with smaller blades for throwing. Last of all, she draped her cloak around herself, hiding her weapons in its shadowy folds. She pulled her hair back and knotted it into a ponytail and pulled her hood up over her head.

There was no mirror to look in, but she knew she was ready.

She found Brit in her own tent, stooped beneath the low ceiling, choosing between halberds. She was covered in plate armor from the shoulders down, polished to brilliance. Brit took each halberd from her inventory in turn, hefting the blade to see how they felt in her hands. Suzanne remembered what Rigel had told her, how fighting made them proficient with individual weapons as well as kinds of weapons.

"Go with that one," Suzanne said, pointing to Brit's first. The axe-blade was smaller than the others, and the pole noticeably shorter. Yet Brit stuck the other halberds back in her inventory without argument.

"You ready?" Brit asked. Suzanne felt Brit's eyes searching her, looking for any uncertainty, any hesitation. She smiled and answered her own question. "Of course you are."

Suzanne spotted Mikayla stepping out of her tent. Mikayla had strapped one sword to her back, and thrust the other through the sash tied around her waist. Her hands were protected by thick fingerless gloves. To Suzanne, Mikayla almost looked like a Pyxian. She definitely had the Pyxian knack for looking unconcerned. *Despite, you know, the fact that we're about to fight for our lives.*

"Let's go," Mikayla said quietly. None of the girls said anything else until they arrived at the dueling grounds. Suzanne reviewed the rules for The Duels while they walked. Both combatants started in the innermost white circle, but as soon as the duel began they could move anywhere within the larger blue one. No one besides the two combatants was allowed to enter the blue circle until the duel ended. The duelists could use anything they already had equipped while they were in the ring, but accessing your inventory meant that you were forfeiting. They could use any special attacks they wanted, but Suzanne didn't think there was much point to that. Using a special move would take time and leave her unguarded, and she knew that if she gave any Altairi champion a window they would take her down.

A duel ended when someone's health bar dipped into the red. Both sides were supposed to stop when that happened. *Supposed to*, Suzanne thought. Those words did not fill her with confidence. She shrugged them aside. That wouldn't matter if she was the one who won.

Suzanne, Brit, and Mikayla met the other Pyxian champions at dueling grounds. The silence of the morning held. Lynx offered them a smile, but the rest maintained their grim expressions. Suzanne took reassurance from the way they waited stoically; it was good to know she wasn't the only one feeling pressure.

Finally, Ramses and his champions arrived. The king led the procession, but he would not lead them into battle. Burgrave walked at his right hand, his expression matching those of the Pyxians. The other Altairi trailed behind.

Suzanne saw Ramses prepare himself for a speech. She could barely suppress her groan. She wanted to get to The Duels and Ramses loved the sound of his own voice. But before the king could begin, Libra held up a hand.

"There was time for talk," she said in a cold voice. "That time has passed. Let us see what these champions of yours are worth."

Anger flashed in Ramses's eyes, but the sardonic smile never left the king's mouth. "Very well," he sneered. "If you're so eager to see your countrymen defeated." He and six of his champions walked to the side of the dueling grounds, leaving Desmond to fight the first duel.

Alphonse stepped forward for the Pyxians. His fingers drummed on the handles of his twin axes as he bounced in place, ready for the fight to begin. The two NPCs approached each other, stopping on opposite sides of the inner ring.

Alphonse dropped to a knee and closed his eyes. His face calmed, as if in prayer or meditation. *He said he had to pay the Altairi back*, Suzanne thought. *Now's his chance.*

As for Desmond, she couldn't figure out what he fought for. But she supposed that hardly mattered at this point. What mattered is that he fought hard and he fought well. The Defender waited until Alphonse finished his ritual, and then the battle began.

Desmond charged forward with his shields in front as a bulwark. He was quick for someone his size, but not as quick as Alphonse. The Pyxian sidestepped the charge and swung an axe at the

Altairi's head. The weapon struck Desmond's helm, ringing it like a bell.

If that fazed the Defender he gave no sign of it. The Altairi lowered his head behind his shields and charged at Alphonse again, and again Alphonse stepped to the side. *What's he thinking?* Suzanne wondered. *That's never going to work.*

A third time Desmond charged and a third time his shields missed Alphonse. Alphonse was free to strike back, but he did so carefully, lashing out and then stepping away, always staying out of range of the Defender. Suzanne had seen the Pyxian cleave a monster in two with a stroke of an axe, but Desmond's armor was much thicker than any monster's. Even though Alphonse was landing all his attacks, none were doing any damage. His most powerful attacks were all Energite-based moves, but Desmond wasn't going to give Alphonse time to charge one of those up.

Suzanne could see Alphonse growing frustrated. He hurled himself at the Defender, battering the unyielding shields with blows that would've crushed any other class. Yet Alphonse wasn't playing defense anymore, and Suzanne realized he had overextended himself right before Desmond spun with a burst of speed and caught the Pyxian under his chin with the lip of his shield. The blow knocked Alphonse off-balance. He barely had time to throw himself out of the way as the larger NPC charged at him. Desmond didn't let up, throwing attack after attack without giving Alphonse time to recover. He drove the Pyxian back, further and further, until Alphonse was standing close to the edge of the circle.

Suzanne realized this had been the Altairi's plan all along. The realization surprised her; Desmond wasn't fighting to defeat Alphonse, but to make the Pyxian forfeit the fight. That wasn't like an NPC at all, but like a gamer. She couldn't see Desmond's face, hidden behind his helm, but she could see the consternation splashed across Alphonse's well enough. Backed up to the edge of the circle he couldn't dodge left or right without stepping out of bounds. Desmond raised a shield and charged.

Suzanne thought it was over. But then Alphonse vaulted Desmond and landed behind the Defender. Alphonse hacked at Desmond's ankles with both of his axes. The Defender couldn't get a shield back to block in time, and the attack cut his feet out from under him. Desmond landed in a crash of shields and armor, and for the first time in the fight, Alphonse seemed to have the advantage.

The Pyxian raced forward to strike a finishing blow as Desmond struggled to his feet.

"He's too slow," Mikayla muttered.

The next moment Suzanne realized she had been talking about Alphonse. Desmond dropped his shield and caught Alphonse's axe-blade in the crook of his arm. His gauntlet pixelated, but the Defender didn't let go of the axe. He wrapped his arms around Alphonse in a bear hug and smashed the Pyxian against his armor. Alphonse struggled, but could not free himself. He rained down strikes on Desmond, but without leverage the attacks bounced off the Altairi's armor.

With a grunt and a twist, Desmond heaved Alphonse up into the air. Suzanne watched as Alphonse fell heavily to the ground, landing just outside the blue circle of the dueling grounds. She heard Ramses's gleeful cackle. Alphonse rose to his feet, but his hands fell limp at his side. The Altairi had won the first of the duels.

Desmond was silent as he rejoined the Altairi. Suzanne knew the NPC wasn't one for speeches, but she expected some sign from him. Even weirder, Samara the Sniper didn't acknowledge her companion as she stepped forward to take his place in the arena. Samara withdrew her bow and equipped a quiver, staring at the Pyxian champions, daring one to step forward.

Suzanne heard the beginnings of one of Ramses's idiotic japes, but she paid him no mind. Alphonse walked over, looking more disconsolate than Suzanne had ever seen an NPC. "I failed," Alphonse said simply, his head hung.

"Raise your eyes," Libra commanded. "Your dismay will not help the rest of us battle. Attend to your wounds and hold your head high. You fought honorably."

But honor doesn't win, Suzanne thought. She kept that to herself. Alphonse looked completely dejected, and despite Libra's words, none of the Pyxians looked much happier. Suzanne was beginning to feel the first prickling of panic herself. Even if she and the other girls won all their fights, if the NPCs all lost then Pyxis would lose. She wouldn't have thought that possible, but seeing Alphonse defeated like this . . . *That fight is over*, she told herself. *Focus on the rest of them.*

"I will fight next," Lynx said. "A Sniper's duel. It will be fitting."

Libra bowed and offered her sister a smile as Lynx equipped her double-bladed naginata. She balanced her weapon's pole over her shoulders, an arm draped over the pole just inside of each blade. Lynx looked fearless—way more confident than Suzanne felt—as she strolled to the center of the dueling grounds.

The two Snipers faced each other, one armed with her naginata, the other with her longbow. Samara's hand was at her quiver, ready to draw. There was a second when they faced each other completely still, sizing each other up. Suzanne blinked and Samara was loosing an arrow. Lynx bent over backwards, ducking the shaft. She swept her naginata around, slicing at Samara's feet, but Samara stepped neatly over the blade, drawing a second arrow.

The second arrow sang toward Lynx's feet and was knocked aside by her twirling weapon. But the distance between the Snipers was too wide for Lynx to counterattack. She blocked another arrow, then another. For every step Lynx took forward, Samara took a step back, always keeping her distance, always circling so she couldn't get backed up to the ring.

Suzanne saw Samara's bow glow. *She's using Energite*, she thought. *This is Lynx's chance.* But Lynx couldn't close the distance before Samara fired off a Double Shot. Lynx deflected the first arrow as a second appeared on Samara's bow without the Altairi drawing it. Lynx threw herself to the ground and dodged the second shot. Unlike Samara, Lynx used Energite constantly to boost her reflexes and reaction time. She just had to end the fight before her reserves ran out.

Samara drew her next arrow and loosed it before Lynx could get back up. The naginata arced upward and sliced the arrow neatly in two.

"Close," Lynx laughed as she stood back up. Samara said nothing in response. She let her bow do the talking and another arrow sang forth. Lynx's hand darted forward. Suzanne could hardly believe what she saw: Lynx was holding the arrow. She had snatched it out of the air.

Then the Pyxian princess threw herself forward, slicing and stabbing with her weapon. She spun and slashed and spun and jabbed, faster and faster, until NPC and naginata blurred into a single whirling frenzy of blades. Samara was within Lynx's range now, forced to roll aside to dodge an overhead strike. She came out of the roll with an arrow drawn, loosed her shot, but the arrow was batted aside as the others had been.

And then, curiously, an arrow flew back. Suzanne realized it was the same arrow Lynx had caught earlier. Samara's arm dropped limply to her side as she looked down in surprise at the shaft sprouting from her shoulder, looking back up just in time to see one of the naginata's blades slam into her face.

The bow fell from Samara's hand. Lynx swung her naginata at the bow and sliced it neatly in two. "It is decided," she said. She was breathing hard yet she held her weapon steady, blade pointed at Samara's throat.

Samara reached for her quiver, drawing an arrow like a knife. Quick as she was, she was years too slow. Lynx drove one end of her naginata into Samara's stomach and claimed the second duel for Pyxis.

Lynx wore a proud grin as she returned to the Pyxians, hugging Libra and clasping arms with Alphonse. "For Pyxis," she said, her voice loud with victory.

Samara still lay in the dirt. The hooded Xenos spoke a quiet word to Desmond, who jogged forward to retrieve his companion. Suzanne wondered why Desmond had to be told to help his friend.

Leo kissed Suzanne on the cheek. "For luck," he whispered. She felt her stomach lurch as he walked into the dueling grounds, wondering if he would fight Burgrave, or maybe the titan Crux. But it was the hooded Xenos who stepped forward.

"Equip your weapon," Leo said. "Let us begin."

"Whenever you are ready," Xenos replied, his voice flat, almost bored. "I am prepared."

Leo shifted his weight from foot to foot and raised his stave. Xenos did not move. Leo stepped forward, feinting a strike at the Altairi's head. Xenos did not move. Leo burned some of his Energite to buff his strength with a spell, and still Xenos did not move.

"Get him," Suzanne said. The words came out as barely a whisper. Suzanne suddenly felt afraid for Leo. She didn't know why but Xenos's inaction made her even more afraid.

Leo turned back toward Xenos and charged at the Altairi. He raised his stave to strike. Then Suzanne wasn't sure what she saw. One moment Xenos stood as still as before, the next his hand was extended, flat, palm pointed down. Leo lay sprawled on the ground, well outside the dueling grounds.

She didn't see Xenos move, didn't see his attack, and apparently, she wasn't the only one. Mikayla stared slack-jawed at Xenos. Even Libra looked surprised. Xenos looked faintly amused.

"What the fuck just happened?" Brit asked no one in particular.

Suzanne didn't have an answer for her. She helped Leo up, digging through her inventory for a healing item. "There is no need," he muttered. "He did not hurt me. He . . . " his voice trailed off as his sisters approached. Neither said anything, but Lynx hugged him as he had hugged her after her victory.

Xenos turned his back on the Pyxians and walked back to the rest of the Altairi. Ramses was blithering some bullshit about the supremacy of Altair; Suzanne couldn't follow him. She was shaking now, consumed by the question of whether or not they would actually be able to win these duels.

Chapter 14

Brit was tired of waiting. She wanted to knock that smile off Ramses's face and maybe knock his head off his shoulders while she was at it. The NPCs were huddled around Leo, trying to console him and tell him it was all right that he lost. But it wasn't. Now the Pyxians had lost two fights and if they lost two more then Ramses would win.

Brit saw Ramses huddle into counsel with Xenos. She couldn't make out what they were saying, but the king kept looking over at the Pyxian champions. Besides Mikayla, only her and Suze and Libra were left for the Pyxians, going up against Burgrave, Crux, the masked Gemini, and that bland-looking Hydrus guy.

"Burgrave," Ramses said. The Altairi counselor nodded and marched to the center of the dueling grounds and stood, waiting patiently for the Pyxian champion.

Ramses was gloating already. Laughing with that hooded freak Xenos, boasting about how the contest was already decided. Well, it wasn't—not if Brit had anything to say about it. Although she wouldn't be doing much talking. Her halberd would speak loud enough.

Brit stepped toward the blue circle that marked the edge of the dueling grounds. She felt a hand grab her. She didn't have to turn around to see who it was.

"Let me go first." Mikayla wasn't asking.

Brit sighed. "Why?"

"You can't run into this angry. You have to fight smart, or do you want to lose?"

"Of course I don't want to lose," Brit almost

snapped. But the look on Mikayla's face stopped her. She had seen Mikayla Watkins look a lot of ways since they had come to Io: scared for herself and her friends, happy at the wonders of the world, and mad at the insanity of it all, but this was the first time Brit had seen Mikayla looking so fierce. Even in the real world, Mikayla was never this sure of herself. Yet, as she stood at the edge of the dueling grounds, her hands resting on the hilts of her swords, she looked positively badass. Brit knew there was no one in this world or any other that she trusted more.

So she didn't say anything back, only gave Mikayla half a smile and a nod and stepped away from the dueling grounds.

Mikayla's expression softened into one of surprise. "You sure?"

"Please," Brit said. "You got this."

She grabbed Mikayla into a hug and repeated the words, "You got this."

Mikayla walked into the center of the circles

smiling. Not a cocky grin, but a confident one. Burgrave stood waiting for her. He shed his grey robe, revealing chain-mail armor covering a hard leather shirt. His scimitar hung from a sword belt, a thin but wide blade made for slicing and not stabbing.

Brit had never seen Burgrave fight, not really, but she knew he was fast, and she knew he had the same whacky perception skill Mikayla had. She felt a finger of doubt press on her and pushed it aside. *She's got this*, she repeated to herself.

"Burgrave," Mikayla said.

"Lady Mikayla," the bald NPC replied, courteous as ever. "It grieves me that we must fight. Yet, you must stand trial for your crimes."

"We did that already. I have a question for you before we start. Do you remember what you told me in Altair? When we were traveling to fight the Lamia?"

"I confess, I do not."

"You told me you wanted to help as many

people as possible. That's why you joined up with Ramses, you said. But if you would really help the people of Io, not just the Altairi, then how can you fight for this king?"

Burgrave stiffened. Brit grinned, despite herself. It had been a while since she'd heard Mikayla get all righteous like this.

"Your parents were Pyxians," Mikayla continued. "You said you would be a Pyxian if they hadn't come to Altair."

"We have a battle to fight," Burgrave said quietly. "Let us fight."

He leapt forward, slashing. He was wickedly fast; even though Mikayla jumped back, Burgrave still scored a hit. Burgrave landed on one foot and lunged again, but this time Mikayla was able to get her swords out. Two blades checked one. For a breath, they stayed with their swords locked, but Mikayla pushed forward and Burgrave danced away.

Then the duel began in earnest. Brit found

herself thinking of the Cheer Squad, memories of watching Mikayla perform at pep rallies and half-time shows. There her arms were wooden, working through a series of gestures, but really just going through the motions. Mikayla the Swiftblade wasn't going through motions, she *was* motion. She was everywhere at once: lunging at Burgrave with one sword while the other came around to block. She was nearly prancing from foot to foot, never still, always looking for an opening.

There didn't seem to be any. Burgrave sliced at her head, turning with his momentum to bring the scimitar around to block her next thrust. He may have been fighting with one sword against two, but each of his strikes were stronger.

They ground each other's health bars down, landing small blows without any major hits. Mikayla didn't flinch when Burgrave's scimitar gashed her shoulder, and Burgrave didn't blink when Mikayla's sword kicked his cheek.

They went on for a quarter of an hour, neither

slowing down. Mikayla was breathing so hard that Brit could see her shoulders rise and fall with every inhale. *She can't keep this up*, Brit realized. Burgrave's face remained set in its impartial mask, as still as it was before the fighting began. He looked like he could go on for hours.

Mikayla lunged forward, stabbing at the NPC with both her blades, but she was far too slow. Burgrave dodged to the side and slashed upward, his scimitar slicing deep into Mikayla's ribs. There was no blood, but all the same Brit felt a nauseating sense of déjà vu.

But Mikayla didn't cry out. She wrapped her arm around the scimitar. The blade cut her arm but she managed to wrench it from Burgrave's grasp. That pulled him a step forward, spitting him on Mikayla's sword. She jammed her other blade into his throat.

"Ahh," he whispered. "I see."

Twice impaled he fell, leaving Mikayla standing as the victor of the fourth duel.

She turned back to the Pyxians and smiled weakly, the scimitar still lodged in her side. Brit ran to her and pulled it out. Mikayla collapsed into her arms.

"What the fuck were you thinking?" Brit asked.

The silly little smile stayed on Mikayla's face. "Had to make an opening," she said. "Any chance you've got a potion?"

Leo ran over and did his War Priest act, transferring some of his health to her. The wound in her ribs disappeared.

"You fool!" Ramses screeched. "Couldn't you see she was baiting you? You opened yourself up to her attack."

Brit saw Ramses standing over the fallen Burgrave, berating him. He was in even worse shape than Mikayla. Brit walked back to the center of the dueling grounds, ignoring the ranting Ramses. From her inventory, she withdrew a health item and used it on Burgrave. His health bar climbed back up to green.

"He lost," she said to Ramses. "Send out your next fighter."

Ramses looked at her with a look of complete malice before his features snapped back to his smug grin. "Of course," he said, his voice light and mocking. "I would not want to keep you waiting. Crux?"

The massive Crux came forward. Brit thought she could feel the ground shudder with every step he took. He stooped and picked up Burgrave like he was a doll.

"No, you dolt!" Ramses shouted. "Fight her!"

Crux nodded slowly, but he still carried Burgrave off to the side of the arena. He also used a healing item on the bald NPC before equipping his massive war hammer. Brit looked down at the halberd in her hands. Compared to Crux's maul it looked like a toothpick.

She knew they were both Dragoons, but when he stood across from her she felt like she might as well have been a Citizen. He had at least two feet on her and he looked twice as wide.

"Are you ready?" he asked in a voice as deep as an earthquake.

"Are you?" She meant to sound tough but couldn't help noticing how small her voice sounded.

He swung his maul. She tried to catch the blow on her halberd, but the pole snapped in half. She found herself holding most of the pole in her left hand, while her right held a bit of pole and the axe-head. She threw what her left hand held at the Altairi Dragoon. It bounced off his armor and burst into pixels.

Fuck, she thought. *This is going to suck.*

There wasn't enough pole left for her to hold the remnant of her halberd two-handed. It was basically an axe, so she charged Crux and swung her weapon like an axe. Crux took her attack and dealt her a crushing blow in her stomach. Brit felt the wind knocked out of her as she was lifted from her feet into the air. A brief moment of weightlessness and then she came crashing back down.

She glanced at her health bar and saw it was halfway gone. Her legs shook as she stood back up, but at least Crux gave her the chance to get back on her feet.

I can't charge him, she realized. Yet she was a Dragoon and that was what Dragoons did. They ran into fights head-on and hammered away until the enemy was down. That's how Brit had been playing the game, even back when she was a Fighter.

But she wasn't some NPC, she was a gamer. And that meant she didn't have to run into that hammer again. Not that she could take another hit if she wanted to.

She crouched, made herself a smaller target. Staying low, she approached Crux again, making sure to stay outside of his range. At first she circled the NPC and he turned with her. He picked up his right foot and she saw her chance. She feinted forward and got him to commit to another overhead strike. But he was off-balance and couldn't put his full power into the swing. She chopped at the head of his maul with her makeshift axe, diverting the blow down into the dirt.

She felt the ground shake but didn't stop, running forward and leaping to punch him in the face. Her hand felt broken, her knuckles bruised, but she reminded herself it wasn't her hand or her knuckles and she couldn't break them. She might not be able to outmuscle Crux, but she could out-think him.

What was it that boxer guy said? Float like a butterfly, sting like a bee? Well, that's what Brit did, buzzing around the massive Dragoon, never staying in one place. She abandoned her normal hack and chop wheelhouse for quick jabs. Crux charged her and she stepped aside like a matador, giving him a quick kick in the ass as he passed.

Crux was getting sloppier, stumbling after her. He swung his war hammer wildly. She ducked under and smashed her axe down on his wrist. He howled in pain as the maul fell from his grip.

Brit clambered up on his back and bashed his head with her axe once, then twice. Crux staggered forward, pawing at his back, but his armor was too bulky for him to reach her. She smashed down the shattered halberd a third and a fourth time. Crux took one more step and fell to his knees. He face-planted onto the white stone and lay there, still.

Brit heard Ramses screaming in fury.

She heard the Pyxian side erupt into cheers and saw Mikayla push herself up to sitting.

But all she could think was, *One more to go, one more to go, one more to go.*

Chapter 15

One more to go. Suzanne cheered with the rest of the Pyxians as Brit climbed off of the fallen Crux and gave Ramses the finger with both hands. Even Mikayla, weak as she still was, managed to sit up and applaud. Leo and Alphonse were cheering the loudest, still stung by their losses. But one more win and it wouldn't matter who among them had lost, because all of Pyxis would win.

Brit returned to the Pyxians, bowing to their applause. Suzanne hugged her, feeling how dented and damaged her armor was. Brit must have seen the concern on Suzanne's face, because she patted her on the back and said, "I'm fine." Then she brushed past to go check on Mikayla.

"Suzanne." Libra was the only one who abstained from cheering. Yet Suzanne could see the ghost of a smile on the queen's face. "Would you fight next?"

Suzanne nodded. Part of her had hoped that she wouldn't have to fight, especially after seeing the damage Brit and Mikayla had taken. But they had beaten two of the strongest NPCs Altair had to offer, she reasoned, and that left either Gemini the masked Assassin or the Sellsword Hydrus for Suzanne to face.

I'm probably fighting whoever's weaker, she thought as she stepped into the white circle. *Ramses is going to save the worst for Libra.* While Desmond dragged Crux back to the rest of the Altairi, Gemini stepped into the center of the arena. Unlike the others, Gemini waited for no order from Ramses. The NPC moved quickly, almost eagerly, to meet Suzanne.

Assassins were an advanced class of Rogue, just like Infiltrators. Only instead of focusing on the stealth aspects of the class, they focused on combat. Still, Suzanne hardly felt like she was at a disadvantage. Having designed the game, she knew every move an Assassin could learn. When she was testing Io by herself, she played as an Assassin. She knew literally every trick Gemini could have up her sleeve. But that didn't mean she could get cocky.

Gemini drew a dagger. The rest of the NPC's body remained shrouded behind a cloak, masking whatever other weapons were there. Suzanne pushed her own cloak back and took out her two daggers. The motion exposed her throwing knives, but she wanted to be able to reach them if necessary.

Silent, Gemini pounced. The NPC's dagger flashed in the sunlight as it stabbed for Suzanne. Suzanne blocked at the wrist and lashed out with her own blade; it cut cloak and nothing else.

She raised a knee to block Gemini's kick and

jabbed at the cloak again, but she might as well have been cutting air. *Aim for the arm*, she told herself. The next time Gemini stabbed at her, Suzanne stabbed at the Altairi's arm. The NPC jerked it away, exposing a bit of torso beneath the cloak. Suzanne dropped her dagger and grabbed one of her throwing knives. It sailed beneath the Assassin's guard and lodged itself in Gemini's side.

Gemini did a back handspring away. The NPC grunted as the throwing knife came clean.

"Can't believe you got me," she said.

Suzanne started. That was first time the NPC had spoken, and Gemini sounded genuinely surprised.

"You should still be attacking," she said. "You had the advantage, you should have taken it. What's wrong, are you scared?"

Ignore her, Suzanne told herself. She threw another knife at Gemini, but this time the Altairi was ready. She swung her cloak up, knocking the knife aside. But that wasn't everything. Suzanne saw an orange orb of glowing light in Gemini's other hand. *A Naphtha Bomb*, Suzanne realized. Almost lazily, Gemini tossed the explosive her way.

Suzanne jumped away and covered her face, but the blast still caught her. She felt her health bar dropping away as she rolled onto her knees. *There's no way she could have charged that bomb so quickly. She must have been prepping that since we started the fight.*

"See, I'm not waiting," Gemini said. Suzanne looked up and got a kick in the face.

Suzanne didn't flinch from the pain but charged forward, grabbing Gemini around the waist. They were almost the same size. Suzanne felt a dagger slash at her back, but she pushed the pain from her mind. With all her strength she lifted Gemini into the air and drove the Assassin into the ground with a suplex.

Suzanne staggered away. She saw she was down to about half of her health. *No good*, she thought.

I can't lose. I made this game, no one's going to beat me at my own game.

"Again you hesitate!" Gemini berated her. "That's no way to get ahead in this world." Suzanne couldn't see Gemini's face or eyes behind her mask, but her voice was heavy with gloating.

"Shut up and fight," Suzanne spat back.

The NPC did so gladly. She ran at Suzanne, stopping short and throwing up her cloak as a blind. Suzanne dived to the side as Gemini's dagger stabbed through. Suzanne grabbed the end of the cloak and pulled, trying to snare the NPC in her own web, but Gemini slashed across the material and the cloak came away in Suzanne's hands.

At least now I know where she is. It was time to attack, Suzanne decided. No hesitation. She tossed a knife at the NPC and charged after it. Gemini turned aside the projectile and met her dagger to dagger. Suzanne felt herself losing ground and disengaged, leaping back out of range as the Assassin slashed forward.

Now's my chance, she thought as she lunged toward the NPC. But Gemini had tricked her. Her dagger found nothing but air, and Gemini's fingers closed around her wrist, pulling Suzanne further off-balance. Gemini's knee nailed Suzanne in the stomach.

Suzanne fell onto the ground. She felt an ache between her shoulders. Reaching back she found the hilt of a dagger, the blade stuck into her back.

Suzanne heard Brit shout, "No!" But there was no denying what had happened. Suzanne hadn't yielded, but she knew she had lost.

"You were supposed to impress me." Gemini laughed, a cold and cruel sound. "So much for that."

It was Leo who helped her back up.

"Are you alright?" he asked. He put his arm over his shoulder. With his support, she managed to take the first, limping steps.

"No," she said. It had all happened so fast. One moment she was charging forward and the next she was flat on the ground. She had lost. She had lost and she had let her friends down. Mikayla and Brit had risked everything and she had hesitated. They had won and she had failed them.

"It will be okay," Leo said. "There is no need to worry."

Suzanne croaked a laugh that was half a sob. "How could you know?" she said.

"All I meant was that Libra will win. I know she will. Then Pyxis will be free and—"

Suzanne would have punched him if she wasn't leaning on him for support. "Who gives a shit about Pyxis? I want to go home."

Leo stopped so abruptly that she stumbled. Suzanne knew she had said too much. *But why should you care?* a voice inside her argued. *Why should you care what an NPC has to say about anything?*

She was relieved when Leo said nothing else. *He'll be pissed later*, she thought, *but if Libra wins we'll be too busy celebrating.* If Libra lost they would have other things to worry about. The other Pyxians engulfed her in reassurances: Lynx assured her that Libra would win, Alphonse swore the Altairi fought with deceit and no shame. Brit had helped Mikayla up to her feet, but neither of her friends offered Suzanne empty words. She knew they were as worried as she was. Once again she felt she had let them down.

Suzanne searched Libra's face for emotion and found none. The queen had not joined in with the other Pyxians' commiserations. Instead, she had prepared herself for battle. The queen's armaments, a pair of inscribed knuckledusters, gleamed on her wrists as she advanced to the center of the dueling grounds. Libra tied her golden hair out of her eyes. Beneath her Pyxian robe was thin leather armor. Hydrus the Sellsword stood waiting with a tight-lipped smile.

She shouldn't be out there, Suzanne thought. *We should be celebrating right now*. She hadn't expected defeat to taste this bitter, but then she hadn't expected to be defeated.

Why aren't they doing anything? she wondered. Neither queen nor Sellsword attacked. At first Suzanne couldn't see what Libra was waiting for, but then she heard a shout of surprise escape from Mikayla. Then she saw.

Hydrus' body wriggled. It undulated, rippling along the arms and legs, torso, and head. His arms deflated and fell slack at his side as his chest bulged, like something writhing within was searching for a way out. Then Hydrus threw his head back and let out a low hiss. Suzanne knew that hiss. She had heard it before, in a dungeon so dark she thought she would never see the sun again. The face of the Sellsword exploded, and from the husk of his body leapt a Lamia.

Its tail was four times the length of any NPC, spliced horribly onto a humanoid upper body. Yet where there should have been skin there were scales. In place of a nose, two slits flared. The eyes were slits as well, blood-red and etched with hate.

"No." The word toppled from Suzanne's mouth, a meaningless rejection of what her eyes saw. But it was wrong. It wasn't wrong like Suzanne and her friends getting experience points for helping NPCs, or even wrong like them being trapped in Io. This was completely outside the bounds of what was possible in the game. It wasn't a glitch or some careless coding on her part, it was simply wrong. They had killed the Lamia—the only Lamia—and even if the game had somehow cloned it, there was no way it would be walking around in the body of a Sellsword. There was no way Ramses would be cackling with glee instead of shouting in fear like the Pyxians. There was no way the monster could be here, and yet, here it was, coiled back, jaws wide, ready to murder the queen of Pyxis. This was no NPC, this was a monster, and monsters could not duel, they could only kill or be killed.

Libra did not balk. "Ramses," she spat, his name

its own curse. The Lamia reared, its fangs dripping with venom. Libra met fang with fist, knocking the monster aside with a savage hook. But the Lamia was a boss monster, not some random spawning to be farmed for experience points. Suzanne programmed the Lamia to take dozens of hits before it died. Entire parties were meant to fight the Lamia, not solo NPCs. It took one of Libra's hits after the other, pursuing her around the arena without slowing. It was all the queen could do to stay out of range, but the monster covered way more ground than she did, and Libra couldn't outmaneuver it forever.

Suddenly, the Lamia's tail coiled around the queen's leg and dragged her from standing. Libra let herself fall, let herself be dragged in. The Lamia lunged at her and the queen knocked it back again. But now she was ensnared, unable to throw her full force into her blows. Her fist connected but did little to deter the ravenous monster.

Its fangs sank into Libra's shoulders. The queen did not cry out. Held up in the air in the mouth of a Lamia, she used its own bite for leverage and dealt a shattering blow to the top of its head. The fangs sank deeper in but the Lamia was dazed. It toppled over and released the queen.

Libra fell too, landing on her bad shoulder. She rose clutching her wound, backing away from the monster. Already the Lamia had recovered, lashing out with its whip-like tail. Libra dodged under and threw an uppercut with her left arm as her right lay lame at her side.

The Lamia's tail snaked around Libra, wrapping her in a crushing embrace. Suzanne could only imagine the damage the queen was taking. Reflexively, she looked away, but she forced herself to look back and watch.

If I hadn't lost. Suzanne was unable to finish the thought. There would be running now. Suzanne and Brit and Mikayla would have to run away from the Altairi and Altair, away from their only way home. It was either that or the so-called justice of Ramses.

The fist of the queen glowed. Like a prayer, Libra pronounced the name of the attack: "Lion's Paw."

The Lamia's slavering jaw was an inch from Libra's face when the Energite-fueled punch connected. Libra's fist tore through the Lamia's chest and burst from its back. The monster screamed. Suzanne knew that scream. It was the same scream she had heard while the first Lamia burned alive in its den. It was the death cry of the defeated monster.

The part of the Lamia surrounding Libra's arm was the first to distort. The distortion spread outward as the monster's body began to crumble into pixels. By the time the distortion reached the Lamia's tail, its torso had collapsed into nothing. Then it was gone, removed from Io as if it had never existed, leaving only a cloud of pixels and the queen of Pyxis behind.

We won. Suzanne could scarcely believe the notion. A roar of celebration rose from the Pyxians.

They had won. The war was over and Ramses vanquished. There would be peace, a Pyxian peace, time to rebuild the kingdom. Suzanne forgot about the real world as she turned to embrace Leo, everything else forgotten. His eyes blazed as she pulled him close.

They kissed. Libra staggered and fell.

Chapter 16

Mikayla had no idea why Libra wanted to see her. Five days after the queen defeated the Lamia, they were still camped on The Floating Eye. Ramses and his retinue fled as soon as the Lamia fell, scampering off to some hideout in the Fenlands. He had broken the sacred laws of the dueling grounds, dishonoring himself and his kingdom, but there were more pressing manners than a shameless king.

On the third day of peace, Mallon sailed down the great waterfall with news of Altair. The kingdom had fallen into chaos; a dozen self-proclaimed kings rose up to claim Ramses's empty seat in

Zenith City. None of these so-called kings had managed to conquer more than a few towns, but already skirmishes had broken out between some of them. Mallon said that they were keeping to their side of the river, though, so at least the rebuilding of Pyxis could begin.

That was the good news. Everything else was bad. It was Leo who had come for her, Leo as pale and gaunt as Mikayla had ever seen him. Mikayla knew he was siphoning off his own health to give to his sister, but it was only a temporary measure. The Lamia's poison crept through the queen, undoing the work of healing items. Suzanne said that poison should be curable, but when Leo tried to cleanse it, nothing happened. Libra was dying. No one said it, but everyone on The Floating Eye knew it to be true. The Pyxians had won peace but lost their queen in the process.

We should go, Mikayla thought. More and more, she was feeling completely useless. All they could do on The Floating Eye was wait for the passing of the queen. It wasn't like she'd have some epiphany that would let her help Libra. This was what Mikayla hated the most about Io. She was so powerful in this world. She could run for hours without getting tired, see over the horizon, and listen to the footsteps of insects. And yet despite that, all she could do now was wait for the time to mourn.

So why send for me?

Walking beside her, Leo was silent. She had heard, with her enhanced perception, Suzanne and the prince having the same tired arguments about nothing. Mikayla liked Leo; he was a little hot-headed, but he always wanted to do right by his people. Still, she couldn't help feeling it was probably for the best if things broke off between him and Suzanne. It wasn't like they would be together forever. There was no way Leo would stack up to the real world. *Hopefully*, she thought.

"My sister," he said, lifting the flap to Libra's tent.

Libra lay on a cot, covered in healing poultices. A second healer had come down with Mallon, joining the Pyxians already on The Floating Eye. The two healers were constantly at the queen's side. But as Mikayla entered, Libra struggled to prop herself up on her elbows. "Please leave us," the queen commanded. Her voice was soft from weakness. After a moment's hesitation, the healers left them alone in the tent.

Mikayla had never been alone with Libra before. Lying down, she looked far less regal. The poison was wasting her away. Her skin was pale and waxy. Mikayla wondered how much of the queen's health bar remained.

"It is good to see you," the queen said. Mikayla wished she could say the same. All she managed in response was a smile.

Libra stared intently at her. "Are you a maker?" the queen asked.

A what? Libra must have seen the confusion on Mikayla's face, because a smile broke out on hers.

"A maker. Were you one of the designers of our world?"

There was no way she could answer Libra's question—how could you tell a queen she was just a character in a game? But Libra must have found the answer she sought in Mikayla's silence. Triumph took its place beside pain in the queen's eyes.

"I suspected it as soon as I met you three girls. Strangers from a distant land, unable to find your way home. I felt myself trusting you three, impulsively, but could not understand why. But now I know. You are visitors from the higher realm."

"Yes." Mikayla couldn't lie when Libra had already guessed the truth.

"What is the higher realm like? Is it beautiful? Or do you fight needless wars and hurt one another there?"

What *was* the real world like? Mikayla felt a little panicked as she tried to remember. It was like trying to remember a dream. Vivid snatches of details came to her: scraping her knee after falling from a bike, her eyes watering and her heart racing as she rode a roller coaster, shoes squeaking on a linoleum hallway, the texture of the beanbag chair in Suzanne's room. She remembered what crying felt like, her eyes burning yet wet all the same. But how could she explain that to a queen who had never shed a tear?

"We have wars," Mikayla answered. It was her chance to speak on all the beauty of her world, but all she could muster was that disappointment. "It's also beautiful," she added lamely.

"I see," the queen said. *But how could you?* Mikayla wondered.

Libra trembled as the poison assaulted her. Mikayla stepped forward to do something, anything, but Libra waved her off. "No. I am sorry to hear of your wars. I had hopes. But no matter. Perhaps it will make what I ask of you easier.

"I ask you not to go home. To forsake the higher

realm for my people. Make them your people. Rule them justly, without thought to yourself."

No way, Mikayla thought. *No way she wants me. I'm not brave like Brit and I don't know a fraction of what Suzanne does. I'm not some queen, I'm just a junior in high school. I just want to go home.*

"Listen to me." Libra's voice grew urgent, ragged. "I have seen you fight. You fight without thought for yourself. Good. A queen must know sacrifice. And I have heard you speak, felt the sway of your words. You will not be alone. My brother and sister, Rigel, Mallon, they will all be here to guide you. But you are the key to our peace. One of the higher realm. I imagine your perspective will be . . . " The queen flinched in pain, but she managed a final word: "Useful."

Libra fell back onto the cot. By the time Mikayla reached her, she was already becoming pixels. All Mikayla could do was hope the queen found solace as her pixelated body climbed upward toward a higher realm.